COTTONWOOD

Summer

A NOVEL BY
JEAN Z. LIEBENTHAL

BOOKCRAFT
Salt Lake City, Utah

Library of Congress Catalog Card Number: 92-70553
ISBN 0-88494-825-0

First Printing, 1992

Printed in the United States of America

Chapter

1

Beverly Simpson and I were as mad as wet hens. We were so put out with our mothers that we wished we were boys so we could join the army if the United States got into the war. We were almost eleven years old and tired of being treated like infants.

"I'll bet they're clear out in the middle of the lake by now, having a good old time," Beverly said, pushing her stick ahead of her on the dirt road. The stick would hit the washboard bumps and skip over the hollows if you handled it right, leaving a stacatto-marked trail. At least, it was something to do. I pushed my long, crooked stick along the other side of the road.

"Yeah, I'll bet they're just rowing those canoes and laughing at us because we can't have any fun," I replied. "Especially Norman Hibbard."

Norman took every opportunity to emphasize the fact that we were nothing but girls, and he seemed to look for things to make fun of.

"I wouldn't be surprised if Mrs. Bartholomew put us back in the first grade," I added.

Beverly switched the long strap of her lunch pail from her left to her right shoulder and tried, unsuccessfully, to bounce the stick off the bumps, using her left hand.

"Maybe they'll bring a baby bottle," she said.

How could our mothers have humiliated us this way! And just because a man they didn't even know had drowned in a boating accident a few weeks before. Everybody else in the fourth-, fifth-, and sixth-grade classes had gone off to the lake to celebrate Wind Valley's last day of school. Only Beverly and I were left behind. To compound the insult, we both knew how to swim.

That our mothers had packed a picnic lunch for us and given us each a quarter was little consolation. Rebellion was in our hearts.

"Listen," I suggested. "Why don't we just go to the store and get our ice-cream cones first."

"Good idea!" Beverly said. "That'll show 'em. We'll eat our dessert before lunch."

Her eyes sparkled wickedly as she added, "Let's take our picnic way up the railroad tracks."

This was almost as brilliant a plan as joining the army. The railroad tracks were out of bounds. Anything might happen to kids who went up the railroad tracks. Not only might you get run over by a train, but you could be kidnapped, or have a bull charge you from the trampled-down section of Miles Webster's fence. Then see if they thought you were a baby!

"I'm glad I'm wearing my red dress," I said, "in case the bull's in the pasture."

The fields that May morning in 1941 stretched flat on either side of us. The earth had been loosened by plows, and harrowed. Some of it had been planted into long miniature hills of potatoes. A few stalks of wild asparagus along the road we walked were turning to seed already.

2

The store was directly ahead, across the forbidden railroad tracks. In the shallow ditch that ran along the borrow pit, pollywogs darted through the sun-warmed water. We watched them, stooping down occasionally to try to catch one while we decided what flavor of ice cream to order.

"I'm having a triple-decker," Beverly said, triumphantly. "A scoop of each kind. Vanilla, strawberry, *and* chocolate."

How daring could you get before lunch!

"Me, too," I answered, in the tone of one not to be outdone in an ice-cream insurrection, "and I just hope Charlie is tending the store instead of Leona."

Everyone knew that Charlie Branson, the storekeeper, doled out much more generous scoops than his wife did.

It turned out that it was Charlie who stood behind the counter, a white linen towel tied around his waist and a pencil stuck behind his ear. Except for Lillian Brownstone he was alone in the store.

Lillian Brownstone seemed always to be in the store, or at least most of the time, telling all the news of Wind Valley and then some. Her neat cream-colored house, which was located right across the street, had had purple petunias planted around its wooden front porch every spring for as long as I could remember, including this one. People said she sewed the best seams on shirt collars of anybody in town.

Her eye raked over us from the tousled hair on our heads to our toes, taking in details to be remembered later, we supposed—how our shoes were scuffed up by our purposely having dragged them over the washboard road in silent protest of our situation, how the muddy water had splashed onto our arms when we tried to catch pollywogs.

"Where you girls headed?" she asked, as we plunked our quarters on the counter and watched Charlie scoop ice cream into our cones.

"We're going up the railroad track for a picnic," Beverly

said. We never told Mrs. Brownstone any more than we needed to.

"What on earth for?" she asked sharply.

"Because our mothers thought the school boating trip was too dangerous," I answered.

Lillian placed her plump hands on her heavy hips.

"Well! Seems to me you'd be safer in a canoe tipped upside down than agoin' up them tracks! What's your mothers thinking of?"

I glanced at Beverly, who probably felt less guilty than I did about letting Mrs. Brownstone assume we had come with our mothers' permission, but wild horses couldn't have dragged the real story out of either of us. We knew she'd tattle. And besides, we'd been told to keep our conversation with her to a minimum.

"What do you mean?" Beverly asked.

"What do I *mean*? What I *mean* is, there's a hardened criminal on the loose. Haven't you heard? Escaped from the reform school last night. And you know yourselfs them bad kids has been known to head down the railroad tracks before."

Beverly and I knew it very well. We'd spent hours and hours sitting out by the tracks waiting for an escapee to come down from the school, which was about eight miles away as the crow flies. We had a burning and never-ending desire to help just such a person get away. But we'd never seen anything but heat waves rising up into the wheat fields, and grasshoppers jumping through the drying grasses. Occasionally during our long vigil a frog would croak, but that was all. The most exciting thing we'd ever seen while waiting for hardened criminals was a skunk.

"*My* mother knows what's dangerous and what isn't, Mrs. Brownstone," Beverly said recklessly, sticking her nose in the air. It didn't hurt to side with your parents momentarily, even if they had let you down.

"Well, just don't say I didn't warn you!" Lillian retorted,

as if the law would hold her personally responsible if we were kidnapped.

Behind the counter, Charlie, who had partially turned his back to us, grinned broadly, and rapidly shook his feather duster over cans of beans on the narrow shelves.

"And whoever heard of starting out a picnic lunch with an ice-cream cone, anyway? It's not healthy!"

With that she bustled out of the store and across the road, giving the door such a hard push that the bell swung jarringly in her wake.

Beverly and I looked at each other and giggled, then ran our tongues all over the surface of our triple-deckers, smoothing out the rough edges that were already beginning to drip. Charlie Branson's face showed no evidence of fear that we might end up as missing persons.

We had all day, so we took our time strolling along the oiled railroad ties between the glistening tracks. On either side of us, in the shallow ravines, layered bunches of willows shimmered with new green leaves, and cattails grew thick. All summer lay ahead, warm and inviting.

On the other side of the world, so far away that we did not really believe it existed, the island of Crete was swarming with German paratroopers in the first great airborne invasion in history.

Beverly Simpson always had the strangest lunches. Nothing simple like my scrambled egg sandwich and apple pie. Inevitably, I was always more fascinated by Beverly's menus than my own, which was odd because she said the very same thing about mine. As a result we often swapped portions of our lunches. We had travelled a long way— pretty close to three miles, we figured—so despite our overindulgence in dessert, we had managed to work up a feeble appetite and a healthy thirst. What I wanted to know was how Beverly's mother had gotten the beefsteak into the thermos jug, because we had a devil of a time getting it out.

"Fried steak!" Beverly exclaimed, embarrassed as usual by her mother's bright idea.

"I like fried steak lots better than cold eggs," I replied, taking my turn poking the fork up into the thermos. The meat smelled good and evoked a brief vision of the Simpsons' sunny kitchen with its blue checked oilcloth table top.

Beverly stuck a knife along one side of the thermos, holding beneath it the little plate her mother had packed, to catch the juice. It was at this inconvenient moment that I saw him.

"Look!"

"Where?" Beverly turned her head in the direction I was facing. Juice from the meat drizzled onto the plate unnoticed.

"'Way up the track," I answered.

We automatically stepped back into the willows. It must be the kidnapper, and we couldn't say we hadn't been warned. We had only ourselves to blame.

"Do you think . . . ?" Beverly whispered, her breath catching with excitement. "*Could* it be the criminal?"

He was gradually getting closer, and I shielded my eyes from the sun with my hand while I studied the distant figure.

"I don't think so," I said, though I had no concrete evidence to the contrary. It was just the way he walked, hurrying along in a sort of helpless way. And, too, I knew that criminals had costumes made of wide black-and-white stripes and a ball and chain around their ankles. "Looks just like the boys at school to me."

There really was very little difference. Even at a distance we could tell he was wearing overalls and a plain cotton shirt. He walked very rapidly, looking nervously around and stopping occasionally to turn and stare for a minute toward the direction he'd come from.

"I think it's him!" Beverly exclaimed, her face flushing. "For once, Lillian Brownstone was right."

It didn't seem possible—that on the only day we'd been on a picnic all spring we'd stumble onto the chance in a lifetime we'd always dreamed about. Let old Norman Hibbard row his boat and laugh all he wanted to!

We were quiet as mice, crouching behind the willows, as the boy in his well-worn clothes hurried toward where we hid. Suddenly he stopped, sniffing the air. The scent of the beefsteak was heavy around us. But he shook his head ruefully after a while, probably thinking he was imagining things.

A peculiar look had come over Beverly's face.

"He's hungry," she whispered. "I'm going to give him my lunch."

"Be quiet!" I whispered back, my voice low, but desperate.

But I knew Beverly. She was a person who rushed in where angels feared to tread. The kind of spunky girl my mother greatly admired.

"Hey!" she called out, impulsively. "You. Want some lunch?"

The boy jumped about five feet into the air, his blond hair flying. Somehow, jumping like that and scared out of his wits, he didn't seem exactly like the criminal sort. I thought by the look on his face that he was sure to have a heart attack.

Not having quite as much luck with high adventure as Beverly seemed to, I cringed even further behind the willows.

Beverly and the boy stared at each other, then she slowly extended the plate of meat.

"Here. You can have it. It isn't poison."

It was easy to see him quickly try to absorb the situation, his mind weighing the obvious, immediate benefit against the equally obvious, crucial drawback.

Self-preservation won out rather quickly, though, and the tall thin boy, after first looking about him to make sure

7

no one else watched, scurried through the cattails and back behind the willow branches with us.

He sat down cross-legged in a little hollow behind a bank and, picking up the steak with his bare hands, began to wolf it down.

"What's your name?" Beverly asked.

"Kent," he answered, chewing fast.

"Kent what?"

"Williamson."

I had guessed it might be "Lefty," or "Spike"—something like that.

I got up enough courage to ask a nice neutral question. "How old are you?"

"Twelve. Be thirteen, come September."

"You ex-caped from the reform school, didn't you?" Beverly asked.

The boy stopped chewing, momentarily, but didn't say a word. He looked back down at the food.

"Oh, it's all right," Beverly assured him. "We're going to hide you from the law. Don't worry about that!"

This whole scenario was traveling a little too fast to suit my less adventurous nature, despite all my past plans of heroically coming to the rescue of a refugee.

"We'd better think this over, Beverly," I protested, weakly. When people started using such terms as "the law," the entire situation took on a different perspective. And Beverly knew just as well as I did that we were supposed to obey the law. We didn't even know what Kent was running away from. He could be a murderer, for all we knew. I'd heard some of those were baby-faced and looked as innocent as could be.

"Think what over?" Beverly asked, impatiently. "He's running away. They're trying to catch him. Do you want them to catch him and put him back in the reform school?"

I didn't want to say so in front of him, but actually, it depended.

"Why did they put you there in the first place?" I asked.

"There was nowhere else for me to go," he said. "My mother died of the smallpox back in Oklahoma when I was little. I don't even remember her. Then my dad left me with my grandma to try to find work. He never came back."

"You mean you don't even know if he's alive?" Beverly asked. The two of us had been reading mystery books.

"Oh, he's alive. But he married another woman who don't like boys very well. He writes me letters every so often. Once he even came to see me."

Somehow that sounded almost sadder than Beverly's version.

"But why aren't you still living with your grandma?" I asked.

"Well, she took sick, too. My aunt out in Oklahoma is tending to her, only she don't like boys very well, either."

"But what did you do to get into the reform school?" I persisted. "Did you get hungry and steal a loaf of bread?"

I'd heard about that, too. How people who really were good people would steal a loaf of bread for their starving children. And Kent did seem like a sort of ordinary person.

"No, I didn't steal nothing. They put me there for no reason. Just because there was no place else for me."

That seemed unlikely. But I tended to believe him anyway, to the extent that I unwrapped my slab of apple pie and handed it to him. I didn't know why.

He looked up, startled.

"You girls aren't gonna have any lunch left if you give it all to me," he said, reaching out for it just the same.

"We're still full from our ice-cream cones," Beverly said, adding her raw carrot and slab of gingerbread to the cause. "Better give him that sandwich, too, Nola," she said. "He'll need supper."

Actually, I was starved by now, but I gave him the sandwich anyway. It seemed my mother had thrown in a couple of wieners left over from the night before, just for good measure. I handed one to Beverly and began munching on the other one.

"Now, we've got to have a plan," Beverly said. "They've thrown him in that old reform school for nothing, and we're going to help him keep out. First of all, we need something to draw a map on."

There was not a scrap of paper anywhere in sight, except for my lunch sack. Beverly noticed that at about the same time I did, and snatched it out of my hand.

"But what'll we write with?" I asked.

That question was easily answered. It seemed that the lunch pail was good for more than thermoses, plates, and silverware. There was a pincushion with needles and thread stuck in it and a gnawed yellow stub of a pencil as well.

Beverly drew a line with intersecting shorter lines to indicate the tracks.

"Now, here we are—right here," she said. "You're going to end up on my dad's three-cornered piece, right by the canal. There's a place just perfect to camp in, and my dad doesn't hardly ever go there because it isn't fit to plant a crop anywhere near."

The boy's blond head almost touched Beverly's curls, also blond, as they studiously leaned over the crumpled, flattened brown paper bag Beverly had spread out on the ground.

"Here's the store," she continued. "Remember, you'd better not let anyone see you around there. Especially this lady in the house across the street. She's looking out for you. So wait until dark to cross by there, and go on this side of the tracks so her dog won't bark too much."

Beverly had always been bossy, a characteristic I'd found more than a little trying in the past, but the value of that same attribute now became apparent. While Beverly worked the whole thing out in her head and on paper, I was still in shock, thinking I must be dreaming. I hadn't an idea in my head.

"My dad's three-cornered piece is about a mile from there. Right after you cross this road."

From where I was I could see big, strongly drawn arrows that Kent couldn't fail to notice with his eyes closed.

"We'll get you more food," Beverly went on. "Nola and I have decided to cook a mulligan stew tonight, and we'll cook it at the three-cornered piece. We'll bring you some covers."

I had participated in no such decision, and was pretty sure my mother wouldn't let the two of us go over a mile away after dark without a bigger boy with us, but things had become so complicated so quickly that I was numb.

Beverly led me up the embankment to the tracks, with a parting word of advice to Kent Williamson.

"Whatever you do, don't get upwind of Lillian Brownstone, or you'll go straight to prison! Oh, and you'd better take these so you can read that map," she added, opening her lunch pail once more. From somewhere, probably under the pin cushion, she dragged out three or four kitchen matches and handed them to the bedraggled young man.

Then we hurried back down the railroad tracks.

Chapter

2

To complicate things, I had to try to fool my grandfather as well as my parents. Grandpa O'Toole had been staying with us off and on since early spring. Times were better than they had been a few years before—we were all pulling out of the Depression. Electricity had finally reached us too, changing our lives forever. We now enjoyed the marvel of radio as well as lights.

This new prosperity had inspired my father to do something about our crowded condition. Of course, he was also inspired by my mother.

"Frank," I had heard her say one night, "it just won't do any longer. Nola is ten years old, almost eleven, and still only a curtain away from those boys. And anyway, there'll *have* to be more space before October."

My mother was expecting a baby in the late autumn, a circumstance that thrilled me. Maybe I'd have a sister, finally, after all these years with nothing but brothers!

My father hadn't known just how to accomplish getting

the money for this project, as there really wasn't a sufficient amount saved for supplies, and he was dead against taking out credit.

"Well, I'll just see what Pa can do," Mother said. "He'll think of something."

My grandfather had adapted to a great many situations. Of Irish descent, he had been reared in Newcastle upon Tyne in northern England, near the border of Scotland. There he had not only mined coal but also of necessity had learned numerous other skills. He could shoe a horse, plow a field, construct a building, play bagpipes, or tell a story— all with equal alacrity. He mastered these skills before he joined the Church and came to Idaho.

Since then he had built two houses, using all sorts of material that included an old boxcar. And, indeed, he did think of something. He roamed around the countryside with his aging horse, Mabel, who pulled a wagon that was beginning to stand out in the increasing traffic of automobiles. He had tried driving my Uncle Rob's car a time or' two but on the second attempt had run it through the gate, all the while pulling hard on the steering wheel and hollering, "Whoa, you rascal, whoa, I say!"

So in the comforting company of old Mabel he scouted around in evenings just before planting started, and he happened onto an old school that was about to be torn down. He bought used bricks and boards for a song and had them trucked from Red Rock to Wind Valley, where he worked piecemeal on the new room, a lean-to, while also running his farm with my bachelor uncle, Rob.

When I got back from the picnic, he was pounding nails in a two-by-four.

"Well, and how were yer picnic, little lady?" he asked, in his heavy accent, removing a nail from between his teeth. "You were gone a good bit o' time. Your ma's been worried."

Right then I knew that the idea of our whomping up a mulligan stew would probably be squelched.

"I guess we just lost track of time, Grandpa," I said. "It was so nice to be out of school."

"Ah, them were the days, all right," he answered, straightening up and gazing out over the brown fields. "Well, better hightail it into the house and volunteer yer service to yer ma; she's mighty busy."

Momma was on the porch, running the last few clothes through the washing machine wringer. She looked up at me sharply.

"Where have you been all day long?" she asked.

As she tossed the last sock in with the pile of clothes, I picked up the basket. Under the circumstances, I decided the best answer was another question.

"Want me to hang these out on the line?"

She nodded, but repeated, "I said, where have you been?"

Darned if I was going to say, "Up the railroad track," but I didn't like deception. It worried me, and nagged continuously at my conscience. Still, that boy hadn't done anything wrong. He didn't deserve to get caught.

"We went to the store, and then we just walked and walked," I answered, which, after all, was the truth.

I hurried out into the sunny late afternoon, carrying the heavy basket of clothes. It was a job I liked doing.

It was fun to pin the shirttails together in neat rows after shaking the wrinkles out with a brisk snap, the way I'd so often watched my mother do. It was an orderly chore, a chore that rewarded you with the sight and smell of immediate, apparent accomplishment. There was something about hanging clothes that seemed to put your thoughts in order, too—to bring you down to earth if your daydreams had taken you too far in their flight.

As I neared the house carrying the empty basket, I noticed that the yard needed work. Leaves from the autumn were spread over the ground, matted and still wet, deep in the shade of the cottonwood trees.

"Momma," I said, after I'd hung the basket on a hook at the side of the back door, "the leaves need raking. Should I tend to them now, or was there something else you wanted me to do?"

"Oh, dear," my mother said, a perplexed frown creasing her forehead, "let me think. Well, the table needs setting, but that yard is a fright . . ."

"I'll set the table first, then," I said.

All the while I was wiping off the table and setting plates on it, I was trying to think. I didn't want to arouse my mother's suspicions by asking the questions that mystified me concerning Kent Williamson, but I was edgy about getting into something over my head if he was lying.

"Momma," I said, laying the knives and forks down by the plates, "somebody told me the silliest thing a while ago."

It was a good time to ask questions, because my mother was concentrating on frosting the cake with light, smooth swipes that wouldn't cause it to crumble. I knew that at this particular moment she wouldn't be so cognizant of what lay beneath the surface of my inquiries.

"What silly thing did they tell you?"

"That sometimes kids get thrown into the reform school for no reason at all. Just because they're orphans or something."

"Uh huh," Momma said, lightly licking the outer edge of her upper lip, while she gave the cake its final flourish.

That let me know she wasn't listening at all.

"Well, do they?"

"Do they what?"

This trait of my mother's drove me to distraction. It wasn't polite at all.

"Do they throw kids in the reform school because they're orphans?" I repeated.

She looked up, startled out of her thoughts, whatever they may have been.

"Yes. Yes, they do, sometimes. There are no orphanages in this part of the country, and sometimes, just to give them a roof over their heads and three square meals a day, they are sent to the reform school. Why?"

That dreaded question, again!

"I don't know; it seemed far-fetched, not a bit fair, that's all."

"Well, life isn't always fair, you know," Momma answered. "Better that they're in the reform school than starving."

I didn't agree at all, but I wasn't about to say anything that would rile my mother. As long as she wasn't digging into particulars, I decided it was best to leave well enough alone. I'd found out what I needed to know, anyway—that Kent Williamson was very likely telling the truth and deserved to be hidden.

But as my mother lifted the cake up onto the cupboard top she added, softly, "Heaven knows I'd like to adopt every single one of those boys, if there were some way—orphans or not."

When we were finishing up the table, she noticed what I'd hoped she wouldn't.

"You haven't set a place for yourself," she said. "Why not? Are you sick?"

"No, just not too hungry. We ate our lunch kind of late."

Actually, I could almost have eaten the salt shaker, since I'd had nothing but an ice-cream cone all day long. But I was still hoping that somehow I could persuade her to let me go on the mulligan. I just didn't know how that could possibly work.

Momma had no more than called the boys and Dad in

to supper than here came Beverly down the road pushing her father's big old three-wheeled cart. When she got to our gate she pushed it down toward the borrow pit and came on into the yard. Momma answered her knock.

"Can Nola go on the mulligan, Mrs. Borden?" I heard her say. I gritted my teeth.

"Come in, Beverly," my mother answered; and she said, loudly, "Nola, I think you'd better come on in here for a minute."

I sauntered into the front room, my mind as blank as it had been earlier, in the willows by the tracks.

"Nola hasn't mentioned a mulligan or anything of the sort to me, Beverly. What's this all about?"

The last remark, accompanied by a rather fierce frown, was directed toward me. But Beverly, glib Beverly, came to my rescue.

"Oh, didn't Nola tell you? Well, my momma and dad felt real bad because I couldn't go boating. And even though we did have a picnic lunch, they thought it wouldn't hurt any to have a mulligan stew too. We won't stay very late . . . but we'll have to wait till dark or it's no fun."

She said this with such a sad face that it was quite apparent that she had, at least to a degree, elicited my mother's sympathy. Beverly was so good at getting people to feel sorry for her. Why couldn't I?

"I don't know," my mother said, rather guardedly. "Dark is dark. I don't like the idea of young girls out alone, and with fire involved."

"Oh, don't worry about us being alone, Mrs. Borden," Beverly said in an overdrawn, compelling tone. "I *knew* it wouldn't be safe for just the two of us. That's why Norman Hibbard's coming with us."

Beverly must have gone out of her mind. She knew full well that asking Norman Hibbard to go anywhere, least of all to a mulligan, was the weirdest thing anybody could dream up if they took all day! Norman drove me absolutely crazy. Oh, he got around my mother the same way Beverly always did. But my father and I were of one mind when it came to Norman Hibbard. We thought he should behave himself even though his mother had died a few years back. People were forever making excuses for the wild things he did. That had nothing to do with it as far as I was concerned. Right was right and wrong was wrong! Didn't Momma think so? I'd asked her that question only a day or so before.

"That's easy to say, when you've always had a mother," she'd answered. "You never know how things feel until you've walked in another man's shoes."

First of all, Norman was not a man. Second, I'd like to know how you could walk in shoes that weren't available to slip on. Try as I might, even with my eyes closed, I couldn't imagine what it would be like without Momma. I told her it was an impossible undertaking.

"Then don't be too quick to judge Norman about something you can't imagine," Momma had said.

So now, of course, Beverly had weakened my mother's resolve in a second way—through Momma's excessive sympathy with Norman. Momma studied our faces a moment; first mine, then Beverly's. You couldn't feel sure, but it looked as though a tear was just about ready to spill down Beverly's cheek.

"I'll ask your father," Momma said. In a moment she returned, a skeptical expression still on her face.

"Dad says you can go if you take Jack along."

Jack was my nine-year-old brother. Old enough, I hoped, to keep our secret.

"And whatever you do, watch that fire!" she added. "Get Norman to handle it—he's almost thirteen and shouldn't have a bit of trouble."

The recipe for mulligan stew varied according to what

was available in the season thereof. The only two unchanging ingredients were spuds and onions. After that, a lot depended on what leftovers were in your refrigerator.

In ours, Beverly and I discovered two more leftover wieners, a couple of carrots, a few tablespoonfuls of macaroni and tomatoes, and a stalk of celery. We loaded these up along with Beverly's chicken fat, bottled beans, and pork chop. Beverly had made a nice nest for them in the bottom of the cart on the worn quilts she'd filched from her parents' attic. Then, along with Jack, we headed across the road to Norman's place.

"How'd you get Norman to go?" I asked, looking sideways at Jack, who as yet did not know the circumstances.

"Oh, I haven't got him to, yet."

"What makes you think you can? He doesn't want to go anywhere with us!"

"Oh, he will, when we tell him we're meeting an escaped convict," Beverly answered.

I scrutinized Jack's demeanor, which had altered considerably.

"He's not really a convict, Jack," I said.

"I'm telling!" Jack replied, turning around and heading back toward home.

Beverly grabbed his shirt sleeve.

"Don't you dare, Jack!" she hissed. "He hasn't done nothing bad. We'll tell you what happened when we get to Hibbards' place."

Nobody had drowned on the boat trip. But Norman was in a bad mood because his dad had gone to a moving picture show with Miss Quince. In his eyes, his dad was going too many places with Miss Quince these days, too many altogether. Norman was ripe to do something defiant, and we were providing the perfect opportunity. Even so, he had to make his position clear.

"I wouldn't do this for fifty dollars unless it was wrong!" he declared. "You'd never catch me goin' on any stupid bonfire thing with girls."

Besides the fact that he felt downright ornery, Norman's curiosity had been piqued to the point of overriding his distaste of girls and their forms of recreation. He accompanied us but made definite rules, one being that we push the cart quite some distance ahead of him, so no passersby would get the wrong idea. Jack, who had by now been appeased, fell back with him.

When we reached the three-cornered piece, twilight had fallen, and Norman began to get into the spirit of the occasion. He gathered dead wood from the clearing and started a bright fire. He even helped us unload the cart, in which he'd placed his contributions—a pillow and a change of clothes. There were numerous other items he'd thrown into a sort of canvas tarp and rolled up. Also, he'd brought the batch of biscuits Miss Quince had made, the ones he wouldn't touch with a ten-foot pole.

Beverly and I threw all the ingredients together in a gallon berry bucket with a quart of water and a handful of salt while Norman poked a flat circle into the center of the coals and then carefully placed the berry bucket on it, using a stick through the handle.

"Oh, isn't this fun?" Beverly exclaimed, clasping her hands and rocking on her toes in the firelight.

The fire felt good. Even in May the air grew cold in a hurry after the sun went down.

"As fun as anything!" I answered.

Norman snorted. Turning to Jack, he mimicked, "Isn't this just *fun*, Jack?"

Jack laughed and poked at the fire with a stick, slopping water onto the fire.

Just after it started to boil, smelling better than Christmas, we saw a shadowy figure walking down the road.

The four of us ran toward it, peering into the darkness.

"Kent?" Beverly said in a hoarse stage whisper.

The figure stopped and stood perfectly still.

"Yes," he finally whispered back. "It's me."

Chapter

3

We couldn't help appreciating our own cleverness. We'd thought of everything Kent could possibly need in order to survive the summer and had brought it all in Beverly's cart. All but food, which, of course, we'd have to smuggle into camp on a day-to-day basis.

Actually, being more of an observer, I had provided nothing noteworthy except my presence. But what Beverly hadn't hidden in the bottom of her cart, Norman had furnished. Such as the long piece of rope he now strung from one birch tree to another.

"This is as good as any tent you could buy!" he exclaimed, throwing a tattered piece of canvas over the rope. "Better than most."

I could tell he'd been paying attention in Scouts. After the canvas had been neatly measured against its other half, Norman pounded some pieces of wood into the ground with his dad's sledgehammer. He then poked holes in the four corners of the canvas with his pocket knife, strung twine through them, and bound the sheet of canvas to the wooden stakes. Beverly and I were impressed, not only because Norman would go out on such a precarious limb for another person, but also because he possessed that sort of know-how. It certainly didn't seem like the Norman Hibbard we knew.

"Here," my brother Jack said, with an air of importance, "let me give you a hand with that."

He knelt on the ground beside Norman, grasping one side of the canvas while Norman tied the twine.

Kent Williamson stood wordlessly to one side, part of his face hidden in the shadows.

Beverly and I were dying to ask questions, but Norman's solemn, studied air, as he and Jack struggled with their homemade shelter, stopped us. We shivered in the darkness, sending fleeting glances across the dancing flames toward the misplaced boy.

"Sure beats that old reform school," he said nervously, at last. "Hope none of you get in any trouble, 'cause of me."

"I love trouble," Norman scoffed, rising to his feet, and dusting off his knees. "I travel with it all the time."

"I love trouble, too," Jack echoed. "Just love it."

This I knew was not true. Jack was actually still afraid of the dark. He just wouldn't admit it in the present company.

Quite frankly, I didn't love trouble. I liked to travel a road with as few bumps as possible, and to lie down at night with an easy conscience. High adventure was beginning to lose its glamour. Even so, a smattering of something lofty and heroic in what we were doing seemed to justify its continued pursuit.

"Have you ever tasted mulligan stew?" I asked, not being able to think of anything more heroic at the moment. "We have plenty, and it's good and hot."

"Smells good," Kent answered. He probably hadn't had a home-cooked meal in months. Nothing but gruel.

I ladled some of the steaming soup into one of my dad's battered metal bowls we used for camping, and handed it to Kent. He sat down on the old fallen tree we'd dragged over by the fire earlier.

I dished up soup for the rest of us, while Norman tore Miss Quince's biscuits in two.

"Here," he said, brusquely. "Hope they ain't poison."

Kent looked at him, and then down at the biscuit, questioningly.

"There's not one thing wrong with that biscuit," Beverly said, carefully spreading butter on each half of hers. "The only thing that's wrong is Norman's jealous as anything of Miss Quince. Since she came along, he can't have his dad all to himself anymore!"

"You pipe down, Beverly Simpson!" Norman said, loudly. "What do you know about the price of cotton?"

Where did Beverly get that kind of gumption? I'd never in a million years have said a word about Miss Quince to Norman, even though I did think he was being silly.

"Best bread I ever ate," Kent said, chewing with obvious enjoyment. "Don't taste poison to me. Wish I had some Miss Quince around to fix this kind of grub."

Even in the half-darkness I could see that Norman was looking somewhat shamefaced, but except for the crackling fire and the sounds of our spoons scraping the bowls a silence had fallen over us. It was the silence that only comes to the country at night in the summer. The pitch-black silence interrupted only by the luminous moon and the myriad stars flung in familiar, astonishing patterns into the earth's ebony ceiling. That, and the monotonous croaking of frogs in the shallow irrigation ditches.

Beverly at last broke the brooding quiet.

"Better get your bed made," she said.

She took the dusty quilts from the cart and busied herself spreading them beneath the tent.

"Now, I put this tent back in these bushes for a reason, see?" Norman said earnestly to Kent. "Nobody's gonna see you from the road, and the willows on the canal bank ought to hide you from Ned Brown's field there."

Kent peered into the darkness as if to verify this information.

"Now, take a swim in the ditch if you're sure nobody's around," Norman continued. "I brought you some soap. We all take our baths in the crick all summer around here. I even got you a swim suit, sort of."

He handed Kent a pair of cut-off worn overalls, a bar of strong Fels-naptha soap, and a towel.

"It's getting cold enough to keep this stew overnight," Beverly said. "You can have it for your breakfast. I brung some bottled peaches, too. That ought to keep you till supper. Between now and then, one of us will bring some more."

By this time we could hardly see our hands in front of our faces. The fire had burned down to embers that were fast becoming ash. I wondered how we'd wrestle Beverly's cumbersome cart down the dark lane, but it seemed she'd brought a flashlight with her. She turned it on, sending slender rays of illumination down the sandy, rutted roadway.

"Well," Norman said, "guess that about does it."

Then he did a most peculiar thing, considering he was Norman; he reached out and shook Kent Williamson's hand.

"Good luck," he said.

Beverly and I almost fainted dead away on the spot.

Despite the fact that I went around looking as innocent as a guilty party possibly could, my mother began to regard me with a suspicion she seemed to make no effort to conceal.

"My," she said one morning after I'd been conferring briefly with Norman Hibbard out in the middle of the road, "but aren't you and Norman Hibbard thick as thieves these days? Beverly Simpson, too."

"Well, you always did want us to make friends with him," I answered, in the defensive tone of voice rightfully accused people so often seem to acquire.

"But I never expected to see it happen overnight, this way!" Momma exclaimed, in a cheery voice with a false ring to it.

I wished Momma would come straight out with what she meant, like my dad always did. Then I wouldn't have to try to guess just how much she knew, if anything. This whole emancipation business was turning into a worrisome, heavy load. It left a taste in my mouth like a spoon with the silver plating worn off. Worst of all, beneath my mother's sarcasm lay real worry—I could feel it.

Ironically, Norman and I had met in the road to discuss how we could manage to run things without arousing just this sort of suspicion.

"There's no way I can get food without my mother finding out," I'd said to him in a stage whisper. "She's not sloppy like Beverly's mother, and I can't seem to find one bite of food she wouldn't miss."

"That ain't my problem," Norman whispered back. "I just haven't got the time. I'm out in the field with Pa all day long now that school's out. Besides, it seems like all we ever eat is hamburger and fried spuds once the summer work starts. And hamburger don't keep very long."

At this point I'd noticed Momma at the window and had rather aimlessly drifted back to our yard, after telling Norman that Beverly and I would manage something.

This was the fifth day of Operation Rescue.

Of all of us, Beverly Simpson had remained the most steadfast. Always on the theatrical side, Beverly thrived on fantasy, quite often having a bit of trouble separating it from fact. Usually she was the heroine of her own scenarios, but in this instance she had thrown herself into the role of rescuer with every bit as much enthusiasm as if she, herself, were the exiled party.

Beverly was bound and determined to last as long as it took to exonerate Kent Williamson. Not too far behind Beverly was Norman. He was the biggest surprise of all. For the first time in all the years he'd pestered and irritated me, I saw Norman paying attention to someone besides himself.

Straggling at the rear was—I hated to admit—myself. And I couldn't decide in my own mind whether I was hampered by conscience or by cowardice. I only knew that I admired those two strong-minded decisive companions, one of whom, until very recently, had been somewhat of a foe, and I felt miserable about my own sense of caution. It must be wonderful to decide upon a course of action without reservation, the way they did, and simply plunge ahead with glee.

My mind kept asking questions. Is this right? Where is it leading to? Should we really be skulking around in this way, hiding things? The old dream I'd cherished of being a spy for my country was dying fast. Obviously, professions fraught with such intrigue were not designed with me in mind.

I scrutinized my mother, who had gone back to her ironing.

"All the beds are made and the dishes washed," I said. "Can I dust later? I want to go over to Beverly's for a while."

"I somehow thought you might," Momma replied, with just the hint of a strange, tiny smile on her lips. "Dust first; then we'll see how long it is until supper time."

"Here, Beverly," I said, handing her the piece of cake

and fried bread I'd saved from the night before. "You can put this with whatever else you've got together."

With great effort, I was managing to save for Kent my portions of whatever food I thought wouldn't spoil.

Beverly looked over her shoulder, then quickly deposited my donation in the brown paper sack on the Simpsons' back porch.

"Let's hurry," she said. "Momma's gone to town, but she'll be back in an hour or so."

"Did you get much?" I asked.

"A can of tuna fish and some cornstarch pudding," she said, also slipping a can opener into the sack. "And a pint of milk I'm keeping cold in the thermos jug."

We crossed the canal that led to the three-cornered piece, going as fast as we could while still keeping our balance on the single narrow board that served as a footbridge. This was not usually a problem, but the sack of lunch complicated matters. Beverly staggered from side to side with its weight, while I followed behind, trying to protect her with my outstretched arms.

With less than a third of the way left to go, she suddenly leaned low over the ditch, her arms circling like slow-moving airplane propellers. Then she fell headfirst into the shallow water. Within seconds, I followed in sympathy.

"Help, help!" she spluttered, coughing and gagging, though she certainly was in no danger. Standing in waist-deep water with her best shoes on (worn to impress her protégé, Kent Williamson), she was perfectly safe. So was I. And very happy that I had decided to go barefoot that afternoon.

Of course, the lunch was demolished. And after removing her ruined shoes, Beverly started searching for the thermos jug, which, should we fail to find it, would most likely catch us up. I gladly joined in the search, which was of short duration, ending with my stubbing my toe on the jug, somehow managing to slice my foot open in the process. This development precluded any further search for the tuna fish and the can opener.

We dragged ourselves to the canal bank.

"Now what?" I asked, tearing off the sash from my dress. I tied it tight around my bleeding foot. The matching sash was already missing anyway. I was hoping for some miraculous solution.

Beverly opened the thermos.

"Didn't even break," she said. "The milk still looks all right."

She stared at the jug a long time, her blond curls looking like strands of wet, unraveled rope. It was the first time I'd sensed any discouragement on her part.

"'Now what?' is right!" she exclaimed. Then buckling her wet shoes, she continued, "Well, I guess now we just give Kent Williamson milk. There's nothing else left."

It was hard to say who looked the most miserable, Kent Williamson or Beverly.

"Well," he said, "you did the best you could."

Beverly watched him tip the thermos up and drink all the milk without stopping.

"We'll try to get you something before morning," she said. "Somehow."

Kent pushed his hands deep into his pockets and stared rather mournfully out over the fields.

"Seems about as much like jail as the reform school," he said, finally. "Except there they had a bed."

"Now, don't you be giving up this easy!" Beverly exclaimed. "Our plan got you this far. All we need to do is decide where you go from here. We just need to get together, all four of us, and make a good plan."

"I wonder how frogs taste cooked," Kent answered.

"Well, if you cook frogs, better do it before dark so no one'll see the fire," Beverly answered, sharply.

"They'll see the smoke, though, before dark," I suggested, proud that for once I'd thought of something worth saying.

But on the way home I couldn't get the picture of Kent out of my mind. Kent, standing there by the flap of the shabby homemade tent looking abandoned and forlorn.

That's why I waved my arms so wildly and hollered when we saw Norman watering the horses right across the fence on our side of the canal. We were far from any houses and could talk nice and loud across the rushing current.

"What happened to you two? Look like a couple of drowned rats!"

"Never mind. We fell in the ditch, that's all," I answered. "But the worst part is we lost Kent Williamson's supper."

"That's girls for you!" Norman chided, with a revolting grin. And just when I'd begun to like him.

"Don't start that kind of talk, Norman Hibbard!" Beverly said, angrily. "We don't have time. There's Kent, starving to death, and all you can do is tease us. All I have to say is, if you don't get him any food, he just won't have any. We're being watched."

We had an idea Clay Hibbard would be dating Miss Quince; it was Saturday night. This meant that of all of us Norman would have the best opportunity to smuggle food to our crestfallen fugitive.

Sure enough, as it began to get dusk I saw Mr. Hibbard drive off. A little while later Norman headed down the road toward the three-cornered piece carrying something in what appeared to be a salt sack.

"Now, where do you think that Norman Hibbard's going all by himself this time of night?" my mother asked.

"Search me," my father said, not looking up from his

book. "A boy might want to do a little fishing, or take a swim."

"I don't see a fishing pole. And he's holding some sort of package." She looked sharply at me, but I just kept drying the last dish over and over.

"Well," she sighed, "I wish Clayton Hibbard would marry Glinnis Quince and get it over with. That boy needs a mother."

"Clay Hibbard now, and then the next week your brother, Rob, I imagine," my father said, laughing. "Louise, Louise! You won't be happy until you get the last bachelor in the world married off."

What we hadn't counted on was waking up to rain on Monday morning.

It didn't really rain much in Wind Valley any time of year, except for quick and rather exciting thunderstorms in midsummer that always had my father looking out of the window in a worried way for fear the wheat would go down. When it did rain, it was during a week or two in April and perhaps another week early in June. But we had either forgotten or never really noticed this unhappy fact.

Through my open window I could hear the rain falling gently and steadily, and from the very sound of it I knew it was the kind that was not going to go away in the near future. Before I so much as opened my eyes, a feeling of awful dread seized me.

The most romantic dreamer who had lived any length of time in the country could not delude himself into thinking a homemade tent could survive this kind of weather.

I reluctantly climbed out of bed and confirmed my fear with one speedy glance out of the window. There was not a square of blue in the sky, nor any sign of whimsical cumulus clouds. It was all just one big soggy blur that had the weird sense of eternity about it.

I dressed hurriedly, ladled a dipper of water into the

wash basin by the kitchen door, and splashed some on my face, glad that Momma was busy frying bacon and wouldn't pay close attention. I knew I looked like death warmed over. I combed my hair, looking first down the road and then over at Norman's house.

"What's so interesting out in the Hibbards' front yard?" my mother asked.

"Nothing. I was just watching the rain; it looks pretty cold."

Momma finished turning the bacon, laid the fork on the spoon-holder, and wiped her hands on her apron. Then she placed one on each of my shoulders. The stance left me no choice but to look up squarely into her eyes.

"Now, what's going on?" she said, her brow creasing. "And let's have the truth."

I licked my dry lips, but the sound of loud knocking on the door mercifully spared me the necessity of replying. My father rose from the kitchen table to answer it, and with my heart hitting the soles of my shoes I heard him say, "Well, if it isn't Clay. And Norman—come in, come in."

Oh, how I wished for the ability to faint dead away like they did in the movies. Unfortunately, I retained full consciousness and just stood there waiting for the world to end.

For a couple of hours I had a reprieve of sorts. Everybody was too busy gathering up Kent Williamson and his borrowed, drenched belongings to get involved with details. Mercy first, justice later.

When it came down to brass tacks, Norman apparently was not such a tough and wicked fellow as he put on. In any event, I was painfully aware that with all my philosophizing I hadn't acted with equal courage when put to the test.

The situation left Clay Hibbard not knowing whether to step on hot sand or a sharp rock.

"On the one hand," he said to my father while Kent Williamson soaked in the warm suds of number three wash tub in my parents' bedroom, "the whole escapade is terrible. I know it's mighty serious business."

His cheeks reddened, and he grinned apologetically.

"On the other hand, he didn't hem-haw around. The minute he got up and saw it was raining, he came straight out with it. 'Pa,' he says to me, 'there's a boy out in that rain. I guess we gotta go get him right away.'"

My father nodded rather noncommittally and, with a frosty stare in my direction, replied, "Well, there's something to be said for that."

"The reason I rang you in on this, Frank, is that I didn't want all the responsibility of having to decide what the next move is. You got any ideas?"

"Well, sure. First thing we have to do is go on up to the store and call Floyd Larson at the reform school and tell him he can stop looking for the boy; we found him. While we're at it we'd probably ought to call Doc Powell and see if he thinks the boy ought to be checked out. Though seems to me he's all right. Louise took his temperature and it's normal."

"Then what, Frank?"

"Then we've got to make up our minds in a hurry whether we want to try to find a place for him or just go ahead and send him back."

This intense discussion gave me the perfect opportunity to sidle through the kitchen—where my mother was making what seemed to be a pretty fancy dinner for Kent Williamson—and out to the back porch to avoid my father's scrutiny. But who should I run into there, sticking nails between his teeth, but Grandpa O'Toole. He removed them from his mouth temporarily to announce, "Wouldna trade places with you for a king's ransom." His eyes could not conceal their merriment. "And was I you, Missy, I'd go back on in there and take me medicine and get t'over with."

How Grandpa could see anything to laugh about was beyond me. Nobody else thought it was a bit funny.

"Nola, come in here this minute!"

This was only about the third time in my life I'd been summoned in that tone of voice. I complied without hesitation.

For what seemed like a year my father simply looked at me without blinking. Then he said stonily, "Sit down."

I sat in a ladylike fashion with my ankles crossed and my hands clasped tightly in my lap.

My father sighed. "I wonder if you know this is serious business? Really serious. Maybe you didn't stop to think that lots of people were worried sick about this Kent Williamson fellow."

By now my mother had come into the living room, as well as Jack and Billy, every one of them looking as sober as a judge. I could hear Grandpa hammering nails in the new addition.

"His grandmother, his friends at the school, not to mention Floyd Larson, the superintendent. Whatever you think, Floyd cares plenty about those boys. It isn't the jail there you imagine. You'd better learn to start trusting grown-ups."

"But Kent trusted the grown-ups," my brother Jack said, suddenly, "and it didn't do no good. They didn't find him a home!"

My parents looked at each other for a long moment.

"Out of the mouths of babes . . . " Momma said, finally.

"I'd appreciate it, Louise, if you'd just be quiet," my father said. He continued to look at me with as stern an expression as I'd ever seen him wear. "Don't ever pull a stunt like this again," he said. "Now go feed the cow a forkful of hay."

My mother patted me on the shoulder as I walked by.

I was in the depths of despair for about twenty minutes, at which time Grandpa came out to the barn and challenged me to a game of checkers.

Chapter

4

My grandfather, knowing I'd outgrown his tales of "little people" from Ireland, had taken to playing checkers with me. Unlike my father, who sometimes let me beat him at the game, Grandpa never allowed himself to be defeated. I had never won a single game in the two years I'd played with him, and when my father let me win, Grandpa would say, "Frank, lad, ye'll never teach her to be a champion that way."

The day Kent Williamson's whereabouts were discovered, Grandpa took three of my kings in one triumphant move. It happened while the superintendent of the reform school was walking through our front-room door. From where we sat at the kitchen table, we could hear everything that was going on but could see nothing. I kept moving my one remaining king back and forth in the safe corner where it couldn't be jumped until such time as Grandpa amassed his imperial army of double-decked black checkers for the final fray.

I knew I was beaten, but Grandpa O'Toole didn't allow any white-flag waving in his games. This was to my advantage that afternoon. I could listen to what was happening in the other room and still profess to be involved in something else.

Shuffling and chair-pulling could be heard from the next room. And then the deep male voices.

"Well, Frank, how are you?"

"Fine, Floyd, just fine."

"You, Clay?"

"Doin' all right, thanks, Floyd."

"Terrible weather today. Guess you're glad for the moisture, though."

"If it doesn't go too far and rot the potato sets in the ground."

They seemed to be missing the point. I moved my king kitty-cornered. Grandpa advanced one of his unnerving troops.

"Well, looks like we've got us quite a situation here, Frank. Your girl was in on this, was she?"

I heard prison doors slam and echo endlessly.

"She thought she was doing what was right. They all did. They're just kids, Floyd. They felt heroic. You remember how that is."

Could this be the same man? The one with the doomsday stare who I thought had permanently banished me from polite society only an hour or so before?

"Oh, I don't think we're going to have to make any sort of hubbub over their part in this. There's plenty of real trouble floating around without going out looking for it. My concern is with what's to become of this boy. I guess you know he has no criminal background whatsoever?"

A third voice entered into the discussion—Clayton Hibbard's. "Sure seems a darn shame, don't it, for a boy to be on the run from an institution when he's done nothing at all that's wrong?"

Our sentiments exactly. But I was visibly relieved by my forgiveness by the law, so much so that I deliberately moved into the path of one of Grandpa's kings, ending the hopeless game once and for all.

"Well, yes, it is a shame, Clay. A real shame. We don't like to have to work it this way—putting a blot on these young fellas' names. But they have to go someplace. If you can think of something better, we'll be every bit as glad as you are."

More sounds of shuffling and shifting. Then Norman's dad's voice again.

"This is a good community. Seems like we should somehow be able to find a place for a young fella in it."

From my position at the table, I could see the road. Though there was little sign of clearing, the rain had let up briefly, enough that Norman, Kent, and Jack had engaged in a brief game of keep-away. The two end players threw the baseball high, out of the reach of the one in the middle. My mother had initiated this so Kent Williamson would not hear his fate being openly discussed.

Shaking his head, apparently in response to my poor performance, my grandfather folded the checker board and placed it and the checkers in the box. But I could tell this was a superficial gesture—he was as interested in the living-room conference as I was.

"We're a little short of space here," Dad said, "but for a while we could put him up. We could set up a cot in the living room, here."

"Why, Frank," Mr. Hibbard said, "that'd be nothing but foolishness. I got a whole house over there with only the two of us rattling around in it."

That was true; the Hibbards had ever so much more room than we did. Their rambling white two-storied house could hold two the size of ours.

"Besides," he continued, "I think it would do Norman

good to have some company. And I need the help. I suppose you could give the boy some work, too, this summer, couldn't you, Frank?"

"You bet I could," my father replied. "I couldn't pay much in the way of wages—a little, maybe—but Louise cooks awful tasty grub. We'd feed him good. I've talked to him about this and he says he's willing to stay with anyone who'll vouch for him."

"But," said Floyd Larson, "we're still going to have to look down the road to the long haul."

"That's right," my father said, "but you know yourself, Floyd, that you hire your boys out to farmers every summer."

"They're usually older, though—at least fifteen."

My father cleared his throat. "Suppose I gave you my word not to overwork the boy or put him in any danger— I'm sure I can speak for Clay as well as myself when I say that."

"You bet!" Mr. Hibbard said.

"Suppose we take responsibility for the summer—have something permanent in mind by the time school starts next fall. Either have a place found for him or turn him on back to the school?"

There was a short silence.

"Well, Frank, your word's as good as your bond with me. The same goes for Clay here. But I can't give you joint responsibility. It'll have to be delegated to a single party."

"Well, if the boy's mainly going to be boarding with me, I'll take it on," Mr. Hibbard said. "He can move in any time. We've got a spare bedroom right up across the hall from Norman's. Do we need to drive up to the school to get his things?"

"That would be a good idea, such as they are," Mr. Larson said. "I'm afraid most of the boys don't have much in the way of personal belongings."

A chair scraped the floor; the consultation was over.

"All right. It's settled, then," Mr. Larson concluded. "Let me know, Clay, if you run into any big problems. I'll be checking with you and we'll get his things together soon as we get back."

My grandfather smiled at me, his eyes twinkling. "Well, I can't sit here wastin' the whole day," he said. "Better go and find me hammer."

We thought Norman would not cotton to Kent's coming to live with him, considering he was an only child with such a resentment against Miss Quince, already. To have a third party enter his life seemed like adding insult to injury. Lillian Brownstone thought so, too.

"My," she exclaimed, as Charlie Branson put her groceries into a cardboard box, "if the whole thing don't beat all! One rapscallion ain't enough to suit Clay Hibbard. He's got to ask for double trouble by takin' in a reform school criminal. Don't know how the man sleeps nights! But one good thing—that Norman ought to get his nose broke good, and none too soon, if you ask me!"

That no one had asked never seemed to occur to her. But Beverly had a thing or two to say right back.

"He's not a reform school criminal, Mrs. Brownstone, he's nothing but a orphan. A poor, helpless orphan." She failed to add that so far he showed more ability to care for himself than the rest of us put together.

Mrs. Brownstone spun sharply toward us, her eyes, as usual, not missing a thing. I hoped none of the licorice stick I was chewing had gotten stuck to my teeth.

"And just who went and told you that?"

"Only Mr. Larson, the superintendent," Beverly answered, smugly.

"And what exactly does 'orphan' mean, if I may ask?"

"Well, in a way I guess he isn't," Beverly said, placing

her hand dramatically over her heart. "His mother died, but his dad just don't seem to care. And what's more, Kent Williamson asked Norman Hibbard's dad if he could go to church with them on Sunday. Mr. Hibbard said he took to the idea of Sunday School the way a duck takes to water. So I guess he can't be all bad."

Lillian continued to stare, but kept any further dooms-day predictions to herself.

"A orphan . . . well, I'll be . . . !" she finally said.

Though I couldn't imagine why, this seemed to make her angry. She grabbed up the box of provisions rather huffily and charged out of the door with it.

Beverly laughed, then stuck her tongue through the hole in the Swiss cheese she'd had Charlie Branson slice for her.

"Someday that mouth of yours will get you into real trouble, young lady," the storekeeper said.

This was less a reprimand than a sort of implied collusion, though, as evidenced by his jocular manner. Beverly did have a way with her.

We too started home into the ripening summer, carrying the groceries we'd purchased for our mothers. It was a warm, peaceful day.

In Russia, airstrips and munitions depots were being bombed by the Nazis.

"Let's go and get us a bum lamb," Norman Hibbard said.

It was a slow time on the farm; Norman and Kent were pretty well caught up with their chores for at least a day or two. There wasn't much to be done except for taking care of the livestock, which they were capable of doing, and irrigating, which they were not.

Beverly and I had spare time as well. We'd helped our mothers plant the gardens and tended the younger children while our mothers tackled the spring housecleaning. We'd beaten rugs that were hung on the clothes lines, till we were blue in the face. Especially me. It was one of the things Momma shouldn't do on account of the baby she was carrying. Beverly always had a little more spare time than I did, because she had two older brothers who did farm work, so her responsibilities were pretty much confined to household chores.

At the moment all of us were experiencing one of those wonderful lulls in the midst of summer. The cottonwoods were leafed out in young green colors, and the new wheat was up and fairly gleaming in the morning sunshine.

We knew the herd of sheep was coming before they became visible by the cloud of dust we could see way down the road. Talbot Richards was moving his herd out to the foothills for the summer.

Often, during the sheep drives, lambs which were not quite well, generally due to a leg injury or malformation, straggled behind. These animals were rejected by the herd and ambled along in the dust bleating plaintively. The sheepherders were glad to get rid of them; they could be had for the asking.

"Think I could get me one, too?" Kent Williamson asked, fervently.

"There probably ain't more than one, if that," Norman answered expansively, with all the pride of an experienced sheep man. "But sure. If there's a bum lamb, he's yours as far as I'm concerned."

Without realizing it, Norman had spoken for us all. I was gravely disappointed, because I'd only had a lamb once before, so long ago that I could hardly remember it, and was hoping this would be my big chance to acquire another. Though I was ashamed of letting such a niggardly attitude overcome me, I was beginning to wonder just how far one must go in making up for another's misfortune.

"That would be just fine; just great!" Kent said.

Of course, Norman was right. I knew it by the look on the homeless boy's face, but I still wanted a lamb of my own.

About a quarter-mile north of our place the main road on which the sheep were travelling intersected ours. We waited at the crossing. We could hear the faint bleating of sheep and the clanking bells some of them wore around their necks. We could see the lead horseman, and two more flanking the herd on either side. As always, there was an inexplicable surge of excitement that accompanied the arrival of the approaching herd.

"Wow!" Kent said. Then he whistled through his teeth impressively.

A short way up, on the other side of the road, I saw the new girl crossing the bridge by the siphon. I'd heard about her but hadn't seen her before. She'd moved here from Sugarville and would be entering sixth grade with Beverly and me in the fall.

"Why don't you and Beverly go ask the new girl to play with you?" Momma had asked a day or two before. But we hadn't gone. We'd been best friends a long time—ever since we could remember—and didn't know whether we'd like the new girl or not.

"Well, you won't know until you meet her," Momma said, and that very afternoon she had sent me with a loaf of freshly baked bread up to the old Bixby place, where the new family was living. As it turned out, the girl had gone into town with her mother, so I'd simply handed the bread in its waxed-paper wrapping to her father and high-tailed it back home. Not finding her home had been a disappointment, however, so now I studied her with interest.

She wore a blue dress and had jet-black hair that was cut short with a straight bang down by her eyebrows. She crossed the bridge and started walking toward us, still on the other side of the road. When she got across from us, she just stood there, glancing at us expectantly, and then turning her attention again to the sheep.

"Hi," Kent said. "We're waiting for the sheep to get here. Come on over."

I suddenly felt possessive of my new friend, Kent, and strangely enough of Norman too. When it came to being around strangers, Norman seemed more like a buddy than usual. I couldn't imagine why; that's just the way it was. But more than anyone, I especially wanted to protect Beverly from her. The girl crossed the road but stopped a few feet short of us.

"Hi," she said, shyly. "My name's Grace Jacobson."

"Well, I'm Kent, and this here's Norman and Nola. The girl with the yellow curly hair is Beverly. We came up here to see if we could get us a lamb to raise."

We all gave cursory nods, as we'd seen our parents do when they met people for the first time. I always made up wonderful statements in my head but they seemed to dissolve into thin air when I most needed them. I didn't say anything, simply continued gazing toward the nearing herd.

"How much will it cost?" Grace asked.

"Oh, they just give 'em away free," Norman answered. It seemed I should say something, but for the life of me I couldn't choke a word out. I just knew she was going to turn into Beverly's best friend and leave me with nobody at all to play with. I could tell by the way Beverly was grinning at her.

We all stood silently, watching the riders nimbly nudging the herd, listening to the men whistling to their sheep dogs.

"I'm going to be in the sixth grade next year," Grace said at last, looking right at me.

"Me, too," I managed.

She put her hands in the pockets of her dress. We all kept watching.

There was one lone straggler as it turned out. He was claimed by Kent, as had earlier been decided. Kent didn't know a lamb from a donkey. So we had to show him how to get a pop bottle and a big black nipple and feed the lamb warm milk out of it. We let Grace watch, too. In fact, maybe the one who was being allowed to watch was me. Here in Mr. Hibbard's barn, the rest of them seemed to form a little circle that I ended up being slightly outside of. I had the distinct feeling there was only room for four. This became increasingly noticeable the longer I analyzed it.

"I don't have a lamb," I said after a while, "but I have a rabbit. Want to come see it, Beverly?"

The girls both looked up, but Beverly answered, "Oh, I've seen that old rabbit of yours a thousand times!"

The lamb had finally caught on to using the bottle and it swallowed the milk rapidly. Everyone was having a wonderful time but me.

"I've got to go home now," I said. Nobody objected.

Whenever I heard people talking about girls who were popular, I knew they meant Beverly Simpson. They always described her to a T. A popular girl was interesting, vivacious, pretty, sprightly, and spirited. Beverly was all these and more. She was also small and agile with delicately wrought bones; femininity personified. All attributes I, myself, appreciated in her. The new girl apparently appreciated them too. Otherwise she wouldn't be spending all her time with Beverly while I did nothing but play kick-the-can with my brothers and hold the hammer for Grandpa O'Toole.

My mother, observing my reaction to the two girls skipping merrily down the road one afternoon, came out on the porch. I wished she would stay inside. Knowing she pitied me made me feel even worse.

"Well, Nola," she said in that falsely perky voice, "let's try to get a little sister for you this time."

"I hope we do, Momma," I replied. But a sister, after all, couldn't help being a sister. It wasn't like a friend, who can stop being a friend whenever they please.

"I'm sure glad you've been helping Pa so much this summer," Mother said. "He's really coming along on the house. Couldn't have done it without your help."

She came toward me, brushing curls from her forehead that had dampened during the floor-scrubbing. She gave me a big hug, and that did make me feel better. I knew she would still want to be my mother even if she had a choice.

"I couldn't have done it, either," she continued. "The way you've done all the lifting for me—and hoed the garden and all. Just like having another grown-up around the place."

She was right about the new addition to the house. Grandpa was making a great deal of progress on what would be my room and the baby's. The walls were up, though the windows were not yet in, and the doorway was framed. It was nice, too, just having Grandpa around. He paid attention to you and was funny, besides. He was full of stories about long-ago days in the old country but you could never be sure which ones were real and which were just stories. He related fact and fantasy in exactly the same way. Like the time he told me about people he knew who kissed the Blarney stone.

"Well, they didn't actually kiss the stone," Momma said, when I told her I wanted to go there and kiss it too so people would like me better.

"Isn't there a Blarney stone? Did he just make it up?"

"Well, there is a Blarney stone, at Blarney Castle. That part is real. I suppose some people have even kissed it, just for fun. But mostly it's just a saying—means you know how to flatter people."

If there had been a real stone with such powers Beverly would have kissed it a million times. Right now she and Grace Jacobson were probably on their way to their embroidery club. The club was meeting every Tuesday and Thursday, I'd heard from Norman Hibbard, who almost split his sides laughing when he told me. They had turned Kent Williamson's camping spot into a sewing circle. Though how they could get a circle out of it with only two members was beyond me.

I went out to the rabbit hutch with a handful of carrot peelings and fed them to my rabbit who, with a miserable lack of creativity on my part, was named Bunny. He quickly slicked them into his mouth and chewed double-time, otherwise giving me his full attention and unconditional devotion. As dissimilar as they were in other ways, bunnies and mothers were a lot alike in that respect.

Chapter

5

Norman must have done something really bad. If not, why would Lillian Brownstone be hurrying up to his doorstep with a parcel under her arm? It must contain incriminating evidence of some sort. I watched Norman's house, waiting for her to come out again, but watching didn't give me a single clue. After a few minutes she hurried down the porch steps and drove off.

Right after she left, Norman, his dad, and Kent Williamson headed out too, toward the field. I stood at the gate watching them disappear into the willows.

"Come over here, would ye, Nola?" my grandfather called. "I need your help."

I sighed as I trudged over to the new room; much as I loved my grandfather, his company was no substitute for my friends, who all seemed too busy for me.

"Hold this can of staples, will ye?" he asked. "We're getting closer to the end every day."

I reached out and took the can of assorted nails.

"Yep," he continued, "pretty soon it'll be time for the skatin' party."

I stared at Grandpa long and hard. Here it was June, and he was talking about skating.

"Ye see that rolled-up linoleum over there," he continued, nodding toward one of the walls. "When I unroll it, it'll still want to curl up. So I says to myself, says I, 'A crowd of boys and girls skatin' on this in their stocking feet would level it right down.' "

He pounded on the staple a while and then looked at me. "You wouldn't know of some young people to invite, would ye? Them two boys, maybe, across the way, and the girls who live up the road?"

"I really don't want to ask them, Grandpa," I answered.

"Oh, don't ye now? Well, then, I guess I'll just have to ask them meself."

The potential embarrassment of such an idea seemed worse than breaking my vow never to speak to any of them again, especially Beverly Simpson.

"Oh, Grandpa," I hurriedly assured him, "I don't think you should—*I'll* ask them. When do you want them to come over?"

"What's wrong with tonight? Your mother told me she'd bake cookies and make a big pitcher o' lemonade any time I was ready to spread out the linoleum, and I think it's as good a day as any." He studied me keenly. "But, if ye don't care to invite them, I'll do it. Won't bother me a bit."

"Never mind, Grandpa," I said, "I will. But only if you'll promise to play your bagpipes for us." My friends were all fascinated by the unusual instrument and were always coaxing me to get my grandfather to play, but being modest by nature, he performed infrequently.

"If they promise not to laugh when I'm warmin' up," Grandpa said. "Sure they want to listen t' all that racket with a straight face?"

"I'm sure," I said.

Grandpa went back to his pounding, not realizing what a touchy predicament this skating party was placing me in.

Kent Williamson had never gone to church in his life. Not just to our church, but to any church. He hadn't the slightest idea of what to expect.

"It's sort of like school," Norman told him. "Only different."

"You have to be reverent," I added.

"What's that mean?"

"Quiet," I said. "You're supposed to think about religious things."

It was easy to see he didn't understand what I was talking about.

We were sitting on the flattened linoleum, eating cookies and drinking lemonade. The skating party had been a tremendous success, except for the fact that Beverly and Grace had left early right after Beverly fell down and skinned her knee. It was hard to believe she'd make such a fuss over a skinned knee when it wasn't even bleeding. She and Grace had spoken to me this time, but in a rather cool manner, I thought.

It had turned dark now and was almost time to go inside. I was glad Norman and Kent had stayed long enough for the refreshments Momma had fixed.

I mulled over the fact that Kent had never been to church—trying to fathom what that would be like.

"Do you have any best clothes?" I asked.

"Yeah, I got a shirt and a pair of trousers that Mrs. Brownstone made. But my shoes are plumb wore out."

So that was the package I'd seen Mrs. Brownstone carrying into Norman's house. She'd gone to all that trouble after calling him a jailbird. It didn't make much sense.

"What else do I need to know about Sunday School?" Kent asked.

"I'm not sure," Norman said. "Better ask Pa."

As the two boys headed out to cross the road, my grandfather called out softly, "Thanks t' ye, boys—and come by again."

He walked out onto the addition, letting the screen door slam behind him.

"The girls left early, did they?" he asked.

"Yes—as soon as Beverly skinned her knee. She had to run right home."

Grandpa patted my shoulder.

"Well, they'll come by again, don't ye worry. Rob's coming tomorrow to take me back to the farm. Want to come wi' us?"

My grandfather called his property "the farm," and my father called our place "the farm." And both men spoke with the same proud spirit of proprietorship when they did. The farm. They both made it sound like poetry.

"Yer grandma would like to see ye," he went on. "She's a lonesome old woman these days, and needing some help with sweeping the floor and such. I'll stay but a couple of days. Want to see if your mother can spare ye?"

Of all things, Uncle Rob drove up the lane with a woman sitting right by him in the front seat of his car! The last I knew, he hadn't gone out with anyone since Norma Jean, the woman he'd been engaged to several years back, eloped with Allen Beezley. I'd heard Grandma say so a dozen times or more. Now here he came with somebody else who didn't resemble Norma Jean in the least. She wasn't as pretty, but she had a nice, pleasant look on her face.

I ran in the house to tell Momma, who quick as anything started tidying up the place, and at the same time muttering, "Rob with a girlfriend—imagine!"

"This is my sister—Louise. Louise, Kate Sutherland," Uncle Rob said, as Momma greeted him on the path where she'd hurried out to meet the visitors. "And this is the pest," he added, pulling a strand of my hair.

"What's your name, honey?"

I could already tell she was nicer than Norma Jean.

"Nola," I said.

"That's a beautiful name. Did you know there's a song named after you?" she asked.

I shook my head, awed by such a splendid thought. Kate Sutherland had completely won me over in two simple sentences. The prospect of visiting at my grandparents' place had become immensely more interesting already. I could sense mixed feelings on my mother's part. Probably because she had sort of picked Marilyn George out for Uncle Rob and was always and forever trying to get him to take her to the movies.

Grandpa seemed surprised, too, as he tipped his cap and fidgeted. But as we followed Miss Sutherland and Uncle Rob out to his car, Grandpa's mouth broke into a grin despite himself, and he winked at me as if to say he'd known about this all along.

Kate Sutherland further endeared herself to me by refusing to go dancing with Uncle Rob until they had first taken me to the Red Rock Drug Store for a chocolate nut sundae. In fact, a strange phenomenon regarding Kate soon became apparent—every time I looked at her she was prettier than the time before.

My grandmother had noticed the same thing.

"That Kate Sutherland grows on you," she told me as we did the supper dishes. "Land, I didn't think she was much to look at when I first met her, but as they say, pretty is as pretty does, and she proves it."

I wondered if Miss Sutherland had taken Grandma for a chocolate nut sundae too. She had certainly done something to make Grandma happy.

"Well, I hope Rob finally settles down," Grandma said, polishing the black top of the kitchen stove. "It's about time."

The sound of a car door slamming woke me up. I heard Uncle Rob open the door but he didn't go straight upstairs, so I got out of bed and went into the living room. He was eating a sandwich in the semi-darkness. The room was lit dimly by the porch light.

"What are you doing up, squirt?" he said. "It's way past your bedtime. I suppose you want some of this grub?"

I nodded. He tore a healthy chunk of bread off and handed it to me.

For a while we ate in silence, then I said, "I'm sure glad you've forgotten Norma Jean."

I couldn't see his face very well, but suddenly he became as quiet as could be. With the crack of light shining through the window onto the floor we both just sat there, listening to the clock ticking.

"What makes you think I've forgotten her?" he finally asked.

"You've got a new girlfriend, haven't you?"

"Yes, I've got a new girlfriend, but that doesn't mean I've forgotten Norma Jean."

"Oh! Well, Grandma said you'd finally got over her."

"She did, huh?" Uncle Rob said, softly. "Well, that's not the same as forgetting somebody. It ain't quite that simple."

"Well, have you? Have you got over Norma Jean?"

Uncle Rob waited a long time before answering. I was glad it was dark, because I could feel my face turning hot.

"Yes," he said, at last. "I guess I've got over her." Then in a lighter, happier tone he repeated, "Yep, I guess I have."

Uncle Rob and Kate Sutherland surprised us all by getting married a couple of weeks later. Uncle Rob had cer-

tainly kept his secret until the last minute. Probably, my
mother said, for fear of being jilted a second time. Most of
us couldn't be there. They went to Salt Lake to the temple,
and nobody except Grandma and Grandpa could afford
such a trip; and more important, Momma had been told by
Doc Powell that Salt Lake City was too far for her to attempt to travel. My Aunt Althea and Uncle Joe Henderson,
who lived in Ogden, joined them for their big day, though.

So as not to feed her disappointment at having to stay
in Wind Valley, Momma planned a party for the couple
when they got back. She asked for, and got, the use of the
church house. Though she'd been thinking in terms of
something rather simple, since her funds were limited,
Ross Elliot got wind of the marriage and showed up on our
doorstep one afternoon with different ideas.

"I heard that old hound dog of a Rob O'Toole finally got
himself hitched," he said, grinning at Momma. "That the
truth, or just one of them wild rumors?"

"No," my mother answered, "it's no rumor. And he's
found himself a wonderful girl this time. Even Ma likes her.
We all do too."

"Did I hear right about you throwing some kind of
shindig for him at the church?"

"I thought I'd have a party, yes," Momma answered.
"Just a modest one."

"No need to be too modest," Ross said, laughing. "That
old scoundrel! Who'd have thought it—we all figured he
was a dyed-in-the-wool bachelor, but he got himself cap-
tured too, did he? I think that calls for a dance, at least,
don't you?"

Momma hesitated. Ross Elliot led the band that played
at almost all the dances in the area, but they charged fifteen
dollars a night. I'd heard her say so to my father just a day
or two before.

"I've talked to the boys, and to Inez, and they all want

to play. No charge. Well, we'll expect lots of cake and ice cream, naturally. How about it? You might remember, Louise, Rob's an old, old friend of mine going clear back to grade school in Red Rock."

"Sure do remember," my mother replied. "Think I could forget your shenanigans? Well, I hate to take welfare, but it's not my place to deprive Rob and Kate, so I'll just thank you and say yes."

My father, when he heard of it, sold a weaner pig so that he could at least pay them something, which was no surprise to anyone. "If Frank Borden had two arms broke he'd still wrestle a bull rather than welch on a debt," I once heard Bill Parker say of him.

As news of the marriage spread through Wind Valley, one sister after another came by our place, offering to make cakes and punch or bring a freezer of ice cream. People in Wind Valley just loved celebrations, especially dances.

I joined in the excitement, not only because of the wedding and my devotion to my new aunt but also because I had learned that my cousin, Peggy Henderson, was coming all the way from Ogden with her folks and would stay on for a week or two after the party was over. Peggy, just a few months younger than I, was a favorite cousin and my number one pen pal.

Strings of twisted crepe paper, pink, green, and white, were draped in patterns around the sidelines of what had been transformed into a dance floor. By Sunday the benches would be pushed from their present position, lining the walls, into rows with an aisle, suitable for church services. But for now the floor was bare and free and ready for dancers.

Two tables were heavily laden with pitchers of red punch and every possible kind of cake—chocolate, sponge, angel food, and white cakes with seven-minute icing and piles of coconut on top.

"Do you think anyone will ask us to dance?" Peggy asked.

"Maybe our dads," I answered. I knew none of the boys our age would do anything but stand on the other side of the dance floor and stuff themselves with cake. Not even Beverly Simpson could get a boy to ask her for a dance. "It doesn't matter, though. It's fun just to watch people and listen to the music. We can eat all the cake we want, and nobody will care how much punch we drink."

Uncle Rob and my new Aunt Kate stood by the small orchestra, whose members were tuning their instruments. He looked happier than I'd ever remembered seeing him, even when he'd been dating Norma Jean. After a number of terrible-sounding squawks and squeaks, Ross Elliot's band brought the notes together in the strains of "I Love You Truly," and Uncle Rob, shaking so badly that I could notice it clear down to the other end of the room, began twirling Kate awkwardly toward the center of the floor. Everyone got up from the sidelines and crowded around them, and when the number was over the men whistled and stomped while the women applauded. The music resumed, and one by one other couples joined the bride and groom circling counter-clockwise around the floor.

"Who's that girl with Beverly Simpson?" Peggy asked me.

"Oh, her name's Grace. She's a new girl. I'd be going around with them if I wanted to, but I don't like her very much."

Nothing would have made me admit I'd been dropped by Beverly. It was much too painful an experience to relate. Peggy visited for a week nearly every summer, and she already knew Beverly had been my best friend since the day we'd been born.

"That's too bad," Peggy said. "I sort of wanted to tell Beverly some things while I'm here."

"Let's go look at the presents," I said, getting uncomfortable with the direction the conversation was taking.

The gifts had all been unwrapped and were displayed on a long table covered with a white cloth, with more crepe paper twisted down the middle. There were lots of pillowcases edged in lace, and egg beaters and water glasses. There were embroidered dish towels and all sizes of mixing bowls. There was a rolling pin and a flour sifter, and dainty glass dishes shaped like apples. I'd never seen so many presents in one place in all my life.

My father, red in the face from a fast waltz with Momma, approached me with an extremely formal bearing, took my hand and said, "May I please have this dance, young lady?"

I had only danced with Dad a few times, and I cherished the opportunity. It not only made me feel grown up, but it was a moment when I seemed to have my father's full attention, when for a few minutes, I, alone, was really important to him.

Peggy's father was dancing with her, too. I foxtrotted right past Beverly Simpson, who was sitting with Grace Jacobson on the bench; and with as broad a gesture as my restricted posture would allow I turned my head the other way.

The boys of all ages, including my brothers, Jack and Billy, helped themselves to another piece of cake.

After a while, Uncle Rob and Aunt Kate left. We ran outside to see if anyone had shivareed them. Sure enough, when they drove off a long string of tin cans rattled in the road behind them.

We went back in to the dance. Married couples, mostly, circled the floor together. Now that the bride and groom had left they all seemed to have momentarily forgotten what brought them there. They were lost in a world of each other that we had no way of understanding. I wished I could be old enough to be circling with them. But Peggy and I just sat on the sidelines waiting for it to turn midnight. Finally that moment came: that moment when the music turned kind of sad and lonely so that a feeling of melancholy welled up in you and you didn't know why. The band was playing "Good-Night, Ladies." Peggy and I walked outside and stood on the steps of the meetinghouse. It seemed we could hear the huge, ancient cottonwoods surrounding us whisper the refrain. "Good-night, ladies," the rustling leaves seemed to whisper, "good-night, good-night . . . good-bye . . . "

People from big cities like Salt Lake City and Ogden didn't seem to know a weed when they saw one. I suppose they thought weeds were some kind of vegetable. Time and time again I showed Peggy what a redroot looked like, and a pigweed. But she didn't seem to recognize them when we walked down the potato rows. And when I pointed one out to her she was likely to break it off instead of pulling it up by the roots, like she was supposed to. Then she'd just leave it lying there, instead of gathering an armful to feed the pigs with.

"Oh, I'm so hot," she'd say. "There's a bee been following me all afternoon! And these awful mosquitoes! I don't know how you stand them all summer."

She reminded me so much of Beverly Simpson that I was not really all that surprised when one day she took off without even asking my father and went to Beverly's house. She didn't even get out to the field at all. I complained bitterly about this outlandish behavior of hers, but to no avail.

"She's a guest," Dad said. "You have to think of it that way. She's not one of my kids so I have no right to ask her to do our work for us. Be glad she helped as long as she did."

Part of the reason he let her off was that she came from Momma's side of the family. He treated that side with the deference usually saved for friends or even strangers.

"She doesn't even know how to weed right," I said. "Just breaks the tops off."

"All the more reason to let her go do what she wants. It might take us a little longer, but we'll get the job done right."

The wisdom of his words showed up a month or so later. Simply by looking, we could tell which of the rows were Peggy's and just where we were in the field when she started going to Beverly's house instead of to work.

One day when I was morosely traveling the length of a spud row with my father and my brother Jack, I saw somebody too far away to be recognizable skirting the edges of the field. Eventually I realized it was Grace Jacobson.

So that's how it was! Now that Beverly was off somewhere with Peggy, Grace would deign to at last come see me. Well, no thank you!

She fell in beside us, on the other side of my row.

"Need any help weeding?" she asked.

"Not really. Can if you want."

She stopped and pulled a couple of pigweeds up by the roots the way you're supposed to.

"I've thought about coming over to your house before, but Beverly said you didn't like to play with girls much. She said you'd rather spend your time feeding Kent Williamson's bum lamb."

So Beverly had stooped to new depths. And here I'd been blaming Grace for something she hadn't even been guilty of doing—stealing my best friend.

"I do like to help feed the lamb," I said, "but I like girls more than I do boys. I don't know why Beverly told you that."

"Do you like to embroider?"

Actually, I despised it. It was tiresome. But I answered, "Sure."

"Want to join our sewing circle, then?"

"You'd better ask Beverly first," I said brusquely, still smarting somewhat from having been excluded to begin with.

"Nobody has to ask Beverly," Grace said. "You and Peggy both come to the three-cornered piece tomorrow after supper."

The next night as soon as we'd washed the dishes, Peggy and I headed for the three-cornered piece, our squares of muslin and loops of embroidery floss clutched in our fists. I was equipped with something else, as well—a wealth of verbal ammunition to use against Beverly Simpson. But much to my dismay, when she saw us she acted exactly as if nothing had ever happened, so I did too.

"Where you been keeping yourself all summer?" she asked me, yawning.

"Been working," I mumbled. She then engaged in scintillating conversation with Peggy while Grace Jacobson showed me how to make French knots for the centers of my daisies.

Chapter

6

We all spent a great deal of time that summer wondering what would become of Kent Williamson. He worked hard, for both my father and Mr. Hibbard. He was unobtrusive, but not really withdrawn. When the occasion required, he could play boys' games right along with the best of them. But he was not uncomfortable with solitude.

"He's sure no talker," my father told Momma. "You purt' near have to milk everything out of him."

"There's nothing wrong with that," Momma answered. "Somebody around this place has to do the listening."

"That little bum lamb they picked up goes everywhere with him. The Hibbard boy has taken to calling him 'Mary.'"

"How does that go over?"

"Well, let me put it this way—I think he's used that handle for the last time. At least, that's what I gathered when I saw the Williamson boy chase him clear down to the end of the field and over the fence. Tore his shirt right off his back."

I too had observed Kent with his lamb. All of us kids out in the country had plenty of pets, but I'd never seen anything quite like the way Kent treated his. He babied it something awful and was so protective that you could hardly come within a hundred yards of it. He named it Rapscallion, in honor of Lillian Brownstone, who at one time or another had put that handle on every boy in Wind Valley.

Among the grown-ups there was talk about Kent Williamson that we couldn't gain access to. But we'd heard enough to know that several people were at least considering giving him a home, even if only temporarily, through the winter. Since we heard snatches of talk, I thought Kent must too, and wondered if he didn't feel humiliated. If he did, we never found out.

The possibility that he might have to go back to the school hung over us, shadowing our summer. Everybody liked Kent. Even Norman Hibbard. Though he had a mind of his own which he made up independently, Kent let Norman do all the bossing up to the point where he trod on Kent's toes. Norman had begun to sense when he was approaching that dangerous area and learned to veer off from it at just the right moment.

Kent didn't have a mean bone in his body. Still, taking on the job of rearing a half-grown boy would place anyone under a mammoth obligation. Not everyone was willing to accept that extra burden. I knew my father wasn't able. But he did do all he could, even using his sparse personal spending money to provide Kent with wages.

"The boy's more than earned them," he said. "Hardest-working kid I ever ran into."

Grandpa agreed. "He sure caught on to the use o' tools in a hurry."

Grandpa had even given him a few of his spare tools. "Ye keep these tools with ye as ye go along, lad, and if nothin' else, they'll provide a livelihood till somethin' more gainful comes by," he told Kent one afternoon while the boy was helping with the house.

It was because of those two, Kent Williamson and Grandpa, that I was able to go back to Ogden for a week with Peggy. They had offered to help Momma with my chores and watch out for her. The other condition that made this marvelous venture possible for me was that my grandmother was riding back with my aunt and uncle as well. She'd be able to escort me most of the way home on the Greyhound bus. After a good deal of debate, my parents had decided I could safely ride the last leg of the journey by myself if I pinned my money inside the sleeve of my dress.

"I'd be surprised if there's any left to pin," my father said, "once she gets a gander at all those stores."

"Well, I'm giving her a little cash, myself, that I've put by," my mother answered. "She deserves it. I told her to get material for two new dresses. She saved almost enough for bus fare on her own, cutting spud sets for Alvin Taylor this spring. Add that to the quarters she's saved tending their kids all winter and she has more than enough. But I told her she needs a dollar or two for spending money. I was sure you'd agree . . . you don't care, do you, Frank?"

With a deep sigh, Dad shook his head. My mother had such a wonderful facility for presenting her cases with ingeniously chosen examples that by the time she was finished he was rarely left with a leg to stand on. And when Momma helped me pack my suitcase the day before we left, she put another silver dollar in the pocket of my best dress.

I tried once again that afternoon to induce Peggy to swim in the canal and like it. As usual, she was willing to get into her suit and ease down into the water to the point where it covered her ankle bone. From there, she'd go no farther.

"Come on in," I begged. "It's warm; once you get wet all over you'll get used to it."

I couldn't fathom why anyone would go swimming in a warm, boring swimming pool they had to pay good money to get into, rather than float down with the current, let the current carry them under the canopy of birches and willow trees, while they watched minuscule whirlpools pull sticks into their centers. Why go to a boring, hot swimming pool that didn't even have the challenge of swimming upstream?

But Peggy stood there, listlessly kicking the water for a few minutes. She went so far as to sprinkle a little on her wrists. Then she walked back to the canal bank and lay sunning in its sand.

Momma never did find out what I spent so many quarters on in Ogden, and Peggy thought it was perfectly ridiculous. "We can't afford to take a bus everywhere we go—if we did we wouldn't have money left for groceries."

So I paid her bus fare too. I persuaded her to take me as far as the bus went and get passes for as far as the connecting bus went and back again to Washington Boulevard, which, as far as I was concerned, was the next thing to paradise. If I hadn't been so busy riding up and down the hill on city buses, I could have spent the entire day at Woolworths and not seen half of what they had in stock. Much of the remainder of my spending money was frittered away on popcorn in picture shows.

"Just smell that!" I exclaimed to Peggy, somewhere between the movie house and the drug store with a mile-long soda fountain.

Peggy halted and sniffed the air. "What? I can't smell a thing."

It couldn't be put into words, but I tried.

"That onion smell and the smell of hamburgers and buses." The distinct perfume of civilization.

She looked at me like I was crazy. No words could express how it simply smelled like things were happening, and if not happening right now were about to. I liked the action of the bus doors opening with that airy sound, the purposeful, almost arrogant motion of the bus driver's arm. There was certainly nothing like this in Wind Valley.

I had bought the material for my dresses and small gifts for everyone in the family. Quarters disappeared awfully fast in Ogden, Utah. I guessed maybe this time we should walk back up the hill and save the bus for another day.

For someone who gave out in such a hurry in the spud field, Peggy took the hill on that hot, June day in good stride. I found that sidewalks were almost as fascinating as buses. This new daily acquaintance with cement and pavement gave rise to all kinds of information.

"Don't step on that crack!" Peggy said. "You'll break your mother's back."

"That's the silliest thing I ever heard of."

"You will, though. And if you step on a line you'll break your mother's clothesline."

Such absurdity defied all logic.

"Who told you?"

"Everyone knows it but you."

Much as I couldn't believe a sidewalk had anything to do with somebody's back two hundred miles away, I obediently dodged all markings of any kind on the sidewalk. Far be it from me to give Momma any more trouble than she already had.

"So, you two finally decided to use Shank's pony," Uncle Joe said. "About shot your wad, have you? Well, it doesn't last long when you go downtown every day of the week. How about a little real work before bedtime? Nola, you know all about farming. How'd you like to give me a hand weeding my cucumbers, while Peggy helps her mother do the dishes?"

After our work was finished we all walked to the intersection to look down into the city at the lights I loved so well. I tried to save the sight of them in my head. This was Utah. This was where my folks' people came from, where most of my great-grandparents finally were able to stop after their long, long journey.

Like my father and grandfather with their farms, I suddenly felt the pride of ownership welling up inside me. My inheritance was an indefinable something that swept through the Utah valley that night, softer than the softest wind, the substance of which was unseen.

It was hard to say good-bye to Peggy; though we only spent a week or two a year together, she seemed like my sister. Her mother had chores for her to do, though, so I had to tell her good-bye on her front porch. She stood there waving until we turned the corner.

"Althea," my grandmother asked, "how soon do we have to be at the station?"

"Well, Ma, we have plenty of time—we only left early so we could have time to visit a while before you go on home."

My grandmother continued, timorously: "I was just wondering if we mightn't have time to drive past the old house on Wilson Lane. You never know when I might get down here to Utah again, and I'd just like to see it once more."

Uncle Joe and Aunt Althea exchanged a quick, impatient glance.

"You know, Betsy, other people are bound to be living there," Uncle Joe said.

"Of course I know it. But I want Nola to see where I used to live. And anyway it can't do anybody any harm to just look at a place, can it?"

Uncle Joe sighed. "Guess not, Betsy," he said.

A new house faced the street on the lot my grandmother felt sure had been hers.

"Well," Uncle Joe said, "looks like they must have torn the old one down, then."

I could tell he was eager to get us to the station so he could go on about his business.

"I'd like to get out and walk around for a minute, Joe," Grandma said. "Would you and Althea like to come with me?"

"Not me!" Joe said. "There are people living there. We can't go barging in on them."

"I'll ask," Grandma said. She turned questioningly to Aunt Althea.

"Unless you think you need help, Ma, I think I'll just stay in the car. Do you?"

"No, I don't need help," Grandma said.

"I'll go with you, Grandma," I said. "I want to."

This was neither condescension nor kindness on my part. I was genuinely curious.

Uncle Joe helped my grandmother out of the car and she took my arm, slowly made her way up the walk to the strange house, and knocked on the door. A woman near the age of my mother answered.

"Please excuse me," Grandma said shyly, "but I have a favor to ask of you. I lived here once, a long time ago, in a little log house. I was born here. Would it bother you too much if I just looked around for a few minutes?"

"Come right on in," the lady said, kindly, "and sit down, won't you?"

"Oh, no, we haven't time," Grandma answered. "We have someone waiting for us out front."

"Well, then, I'll walk around back with you. The old house is still there. No one lives in it, of course—we're using it for a shed. But come on, I'll show you."

She stood with us for a minute or two in front of the very old building, so old that the roof seemed to have dented in the middle. Then she said: "Well, here it is. Take your time; stay as long as you like."

My grandmother placed her hand against one of the logs, slowly tracing its ridges and moving on to the dusty, cracked pane of glass in one of the tiny square window frames.

I stood silently beside her. After a while she took my hand lightly, the way one of my friends might, and started walking with me down a footpath that wound through a patch of wildwood.

"Here is where I used to play—usually all by myself. Oh, now and then John or Arthur would play a game with me. And then, for a month or so a girl my age lived in a house that used to be over there in that pasture. Her name was Jessie Bingham. But something happened, I never did know what, and she moved away."

I felt that my grandmother had almost forgotten I was walking with her, listening, but suddenly she looked down at me and smiled and said: "You should have seen the clothes we wore. Our skirts came clear down to our ankles. But that didn't stop us running almost as fast as the boys."

"Why did you move away, Grandma?" I asked.

She looked startled by the question.

"Why, because of the Manifesto. We were the second family. Hasn't your mother told you?"

I'd heard that my grandmother had lived in a plural marriage family, but I had not realized how that was related to the move to Idaho.

"Yes. My father had to choose one family to stay with and he thought his main responsibility was with the first."

"So what did you do, Grandma? I mean for a living?"

"Oh, he bought a small farm for us in Red Rock, just a mile or so from where we live now. And besides me there were the two older brothers, you know. We all farmed it, together. And I soon found work in the winter as a hired girl. My brother would drive me in on a hay wagon late in the fall and I'd board with people until about the middle of April."

"Tell me more about your clothes, Grandma," I said.

"We wore black stockings. Ugly black stockings, and high shoes. And over our dresses we wore pinafores. Know what a pinafore is?"

I shook my head, still holding her hand.

"It's like an apron. They were usually white. And we wore our hair long and tied back."

She stood scanning the fields with eyes that suddenly looked vigorous and young.

The lady came out of her house and handed a glass to my grandmother.

"I thought you might like a drink of water," she said. "I'd be glad to bring a chair out for you to sit on."

"Thanks, but we have to be going along," Grandma said. "We won't be staying long—I'd just like to stand here for a bit, if you don't mind."

"Not at all," the lady said. "I'm glad you could come by. Come again any time."

She went back into her house and left us alone with the fields. I followed my grandmother's gaze, which seemed to cover a tremendous distance.

For a moment I imagined I saw ghosts of girls in black stockings and pinafores ducking in and out of the trees way down at the end of the path, and I was quite sure from the look on my grandmother's face that she must have seen them too.

"I wish I could have been your friend back then, Grandma," I said. "I would have played with you. I think we'd have been the best friends ever."

"Why, Nola," she said, smiling in a sad sort of way, "that's the nicest thing anyone's ever said to me."

Norman pitched the ball so fast that it almost hit me in the head as it sped by. It landed in Jack's mitt with a terrific thwack. It wasn't the first wild ball he'd thrown that afternoon, either. He was obviously in one of his moods.

"What's eating you?" Jack demanded angrily. "Knock a guy's glove right outta his hand, why don't you?"

"Whatcha playin' for, if you can't take it?" Norman replied, throwing his glove on the ground and kicking it a couple of times. It was a pretty bad performance, even for Norman. In fact, it was the first serious outburst we'd seen since Kent Williamson had started boarding with the Hibbards. Because we'd gotten used to a better-behaved Norman, the effect was all the more startling.

"Yeah, Norman," Beverly joined in. "What *is* eating you? Bet it has something to do with that Miss Quince."

"Well, what if it has?"

He now had our undivided attention.

"What's Miss Quince done now?" I asked.

"What she's done is gone and got my Pa to propose to her. And ain't one thing I can do about it. Not one thing."

Not that he hadn't tried. We later learned from Kent Williamson that upon discovering his father's intentions, Norman had made a proposal of his own.

"Let's run away and join the circus, Kent—today!"

Kent, however, preferred the farm to soggy homemade tents, and Glinnis Quince's hot apple pie to rebellion.

"I've run as far as I want to go for a while," he said to Norman. "I'd just as leave stay right here as long as I can. I've got bacon to eat, a good warm bed, and I've even saved twenty-three dollars. It'd be dumb to walk away from a deal like that."

The other unavoidable barrier to this plot of Norman's was the lack of a circus to join. As far as anyone could remember, no circus had ever come anyplace near Wind Valley before, and it wasn't likely to now just because Norman wanted it to.

What he had said was true, though. His father was going to marry Glinnis Quince and there was nothing Norman could do about it. What was worse, nobody in the world was on his side. The whole valley was tickled to death with the prospect of Clayton Hibbard getting married again at last.

"Why can't you be glad?" Kent kept asking him. "Why can't you just stop being so ornery and just be glad for hot apple pie and fried chicken? And think of all the dishes we won't have to wash. Doesn't that count for anything?"

"We never needed a woman around all these years," Norman blustered. "We did fine. Why should we need one now?"

Clay Hibbard didn't know what to make of it. I was sitting up in the branches of the red astrakhan tree trying to find out if the green apples were big enough to eat without getting a stomach ache when I heard him talking to my dad.

"Frank, I don't know what to do with the boy. He's dead set against my getting married to Glinnis. And she's been good as gold to him. Nobody could have treated a boy better. I've racked my brain over it."

My father got out his pocket knife and started whittling on a stick. He liked to do that when he had a problem; he said whittling made him think better.

"Well, Clay," he said at last, "don't know as I'm the one to advise you, never having had your situation, but I believe I'd explain to him how a man needs companionship. Then if he threw another one of his tantrums I'd just tell him to go whistle in the wind."

I could see, through the leaves, my father look up from his stick and grin at the other man.

"You know, Clay," he continued. "As long as he thinks it's bothering you, he's gonna keep it up. If I was you, I'd just ignore him entirely. You've done a fine job of raising that boy all by yourself. Everybody knows that. But maybe, in a way, you've tried too hard. It's easy for a man to do that. I know from experience."

73

I tried to think of an example of my father's trying too hard to be too easy on us. None came readily to mind.

"Sounds like good advice, Frank. I believe you're right."

"Just make sure you don't let him bamboozle you into losing a fine woman like Glinnis. You'd always be sorry you did," Dad continued. "Norman's gonna be all grown up and out of the nest in what—five, six years? Think *he's* gonna go without a wife then, on *your* account?"

"Well, no. I wouldn't want him to."

"'Course not. Looking back on it, that's not what he'll want for you, either. Probably feel mighty guilty, I'd expect."

Mr. Hibbard stood up nice and straight and tucked his loose shirttail in purposefully. "You're absolutely right, Frank. I'm still the boss around that place," he said.

That day the Luftwaffe struck Moscow with two hundred planes in waves at half-hour intervals for five and one-half hours.

No matter what the weather was like any other day—windy or electric with beautiful, violent thunderstorms—on the twenty-fourth of July it was always hot and still. The fact that this condition in climate never varied was downright awe-inspiring. Especially if you were on a float with the sun beating down on you.

This time I was at least dressed for the part, and I had actually benefited from being a foot taller than Beverly and eight inches taller than Grace, who were posing as my children. I was used to this role. Everyone knew mothers were taller than children, except in the case of my mother. I had already passed her up. At present I was playing the part of a pioneer woman all outfitted in a sunbonnet, which, I was learning first-hand, really did help you keep from melting clear away.

No matter what I did I couldn't escape from sagebrush.

Wind Valley Ward had taken advantage of its natural props, saving both time and money. I sat at a spinning wheel, doing no better with spinning than with embroidering. But I was better off than Beverly and Grace, who had to stand and smile into the sun.

Our float had one rather incongruous feature—my grandfather. Though the rest of us were pioneers, the residents of Wind Valley couldn't see wasting Grandpa's talent at bagpipe playing. Of particular interest was his outstanding costume, which included a kilt.

So there he stood in his kilt, his flat black Tam o' Shanter pulled to a rakish angle on his head, playing all kinds of tunes; religious songs, marches, Irish jigs, or sentimental Irish ballads—whatever came into his head. Always his performance brought a wave of enthusiastic applause, to which he'd bow in a dignified, old-worldly way.

They sat him in one corner on a chair beneath an umbrella labelled Irish Pioneer.

Hot as it was, you could feel something creeping into summer. The newness of it, the lush greenness, was starting to slip away into August, which was a month that seemed to wait in limbo for autumn to arrive.

The horses that pulled our float along the paved road smelled strong and dusty. Close by me Kent Williamson stood holding my father's pitchfork and wearing one of Dad's old battered felt hats. He'd not so much as seen a Pioneer Day parade, let alone been in one, and was having the time of his life. Norman roasted next to him in a coonskin cap. The hay was cut, the gardens had recently been weeded, and we all had two days off.

"Next thing you know," I said, trying not to move my lips, "we'll have to be thinking of buying our school stuff." I could have bitten my tongue when I saw the look that came over Kent Williamson's face.

"Wonder where I'll be going to school," he said.

There had been a lot of talk about taking him in, but still nobody was putting his money where his mouth was on this.

"You'll be going right in Wind Valley with the rest of us," I said with a bravado that was not genuine.

"I hope so," he said. "Feel more at home there than I have anyplace since Grandma's."

I gave my spinning wheel a hard turn and it fell over on my bare foot. I didn't mind; it got everybody's attention off what I'd blundered into.

Chapter

7

Three is not the most desirable number for smooth relationships. Even so, Beverly, Grace, and I managed to improve our skills in coping with it. After the first blow to my life-long exclusive friendship with Beverly, I began to gradually appreciate variety. Grace Jacobson was altogether different from Beverly, and often a welcome change. For one thing, she frequently asked me what I wanted to do instead of automatically making my decisions for me. Along with that, she lent a quiet strength to my naturally backward temperament. In short, when Beverly acted up we were two against one.

"Well, me lads and lasses," Grandpa said, "just look what we've accomplished."

He took a few steps backward and wiped his brow with his shirt sleeve. We were all helping to complete the new addition. The room was finished and only needed painting inside and out. I would soon have a place all my own.

He had everyone helping him—Grace, Beverly, and the

two boys from across the way. We were making something of a minor celebration of the near-completion of our task, and it was in the midst of this celebration that I began to realize that my grandfather wouldn't be staying at our place much longer. I started missing him before he'd even gone.

"I know what it is ye all need," he suddenly said. "Ye all need some root beer. We'll have to find a ride up to the store. Who could you think of we could finagle into gettin' us there?"

The obvious choice was Momma, who, like her father, heartily enjoyed a diversion, however small, and root beer too. She crammed us two-deep into the back seat of the car and we headed down the road.

"Well, when's the weddin' to be, then?" Grandpa said, turning from his front-seat place to face Norman Hibbard.

"Ain't decided," he mumbled. "Far as I'm concerned, never."

"Now, why would a good lad the likes of you be sayin' such a poor word?" Grandpa asked, an expression of exaggerated disappointment altering his features. "Imagine a young feller begrudging good people what they only deserve. 'Tisn't like ye, even. Can't believe it of a boy who's been willing to help me the way you have the past day or two. And for next to nothing in wages. Couldna ye be just half as generous with your own dad?"

Norman stared out of the window at the road, a sullen look on his face.

"Would ye be answering me, lad?" Grandpa persisted.

"Don't matter to me when they get hitched," Norman snapped.

"Well, why don't ye help 'em out a bit. You know, you can act glad even if you don't feel it. Practice makes perfect—ever heard the sayin'? Works, too. Act glad for your father long enough and the day might come when you see this in a different light."

"Maybe," Norman said, continuing to glower. He didn't dare lose his temper in response to anyone my grandfather's age. But I heard him whisper to himself, "and maybe not."

"Look at it this way, son: you got yourself a friend here in Kent. Don't you enjoy having him stay at your place?"

"Why, sure."

"Well, grown people need one another's company, too." He paused, waiting for the light to dawn on Norman; but Norman, whose face had become beet-red, went on sulking.

Grandpa sighed. "Ah, well. I'm just an old man and should mind me own business."

Norman validated the statement by remaining silent.

Though all of us had made friends that summer because of Kent Williamson coming into our lives, whenever we entered a public place such as the store, we separated—the girls standing by the candy case and the boys naturally gravitating toward the back, where such items as razor blades and work gloves were stacked. I had noticed that their fathers did the same thing, posturing the same way with their hands on their hips.

"Here you go, young fellers." My grandfather beamed as he handed out his treat. He was a great one for creating an occasion. After a few minutes, when the pop was about half gone, my mother came up beside him and put her hand on his arm.

"Pa," she said, hesitantly, "I think you must have forgotten to pay Charlie."

A strange look came over Grandpa's face. He took his coin purse out of his pocket, looked at it, put it in his pocket again, and looked at my mother in a bemused way. She returned his questioning stare and then softly said, "Just hand your purse to me, Pa. I'll take care of it."

I didn't understand what was happening, but I knew something was. I thought maybe I should get everybody out of there, so I walked over to where Grace and Beverly were.

"Let's go see if the train is coming," I said. Then in a louder voice to the boys, "Race you out to the tracks!"

We ran across the street; the boys followed close behind, purposely fizzing up their bottles of pop. When I got to the railroad tracks I didn't stop to put my ear down to listen for the train. I just kept running, faster and faster along the railroad ties.

Our club continued to meet at the three-cornered piece, but it changed from an embroidery club to a basket-weaving club, an entirely unsuccessful enterprise. When my turn came to sponsor the rotating organization, we became a book-reading club. Success was ensured in a book-reading club, as we had only to rely on the skills of others. Still, Beverly Simpson was disheartened.

"The last part of summer, and all you want to do is read old books! Might as well have an arithmetic club while we're at it."

Though I'd felt a book-reading club was a good enough idea, my interest was waning, too. The collective mass of boys had started pestering us all through our meetings; hiding in the willows and doing juvenile bits of mischief such as throwing water-filled bags at us. Kent Williamson was getting to be as bad as the rest of them. In fact, it seemed that summer was lasting too long. I was tired of tromping hay. I was tired of picking peas. I was eager for the smell of five-cent tablets and artgum erasers. Just in time, the Oakleys rescued me from my midsummer ennui.

We had just finished eating supper one evening; my father had gone out on the front steps to whittle while Momma and I did the dishes. Momma was getting big and the hot weather was wearing her out.

"Why don't you go on out with Dad," I said. "It's cool out there. I can finish up."

Momma cast a grateful look my way.

"Why, thanks, honey. I think I'll take you up on that."

I listened to their murmuring voices while I scrubbed the table top. I couldn't make out the words, but the sound was warm and comforting. Suddenly Dad's voice changed.

"Well, for ever more!" he said, laughing. "If it isn't a band of those darned gypsies."

I threw the wet cloth into the dishpan and ran out on the porch. The next thing I knew, Aunt Ida was squeezing the life out of my dad while Audra was squeezing the life out of me.

The Oakleys were my cousins. They were from my father's side of the family; the side we rarely saw. You would never guess that, though, to watch Aunt Ida give my father a big smacking kiss on the cheek.

"Oh, Frank, you little beggar—you get better-looking every time I see you!" she exclaimed, with a deep, throaty chuckle. "Always were the handsomest one of the bunch."

This was the way the Oakleys were. They blew in from nowhere without warning and acted as if they had seen you only the day before, though actually it would have been about five years.

"We're sort of stranded here, Frank," Sylvan Oakley said. For reasons unknown to me, my father's brother-in-law was never referred to as Uncle Sylvan or even plain Sylvan. He was always called Sylvan Oakley. Perhaps the family didn't quite approve of him, though of all my uncles he was the most colorful and amusing.

"How do you mean?" Dad asked.

"Well, we started out for Yellowstone Park and who knows, we might make it there yet. We just made up our minds if we waited till we could afford it we'd sit on Goshen Street the rest of our lives. I patched up about a dozen or so tires I collected from the junk yards and we've gone through at least half of them gettin' this far."

"You're staying here tonight," Momma said. "Don't even

think of doing anything else. We'll spread quilts out on the floor of the front room for the kids and you can have our bed. Frank and I will sleep in the new room."

But Sylvan Oakley held his hand up in protest.

"Wouldn't dream of it, Louise. Thanks just the same, but we've got our gear with us. If we can just camp out under the apple trees we'll make out fine. Got ham and eggs enough for an army. But I would take some of that leaf lettuce in your garden, if you twisted my arm."

Parked out front was the Oakleys' truck, so old and wobbly that I was surprised a tire would stay on it long enough to go flat. All kinds of items were sort of roped together on top of the truck bed, which also served as the riding place for my six Oakley cousins, all older boys except Audra, who was not too much older than I. I could remember her only slightly, but she soon reminded me of activities we'd both engaged in during their last visit.

"It was so much fun when we all went fishing and picked those chokecherries, wasn't it? I'd sure like some of that chokecherry jelly. Momma says the season might not be over yet. Think we could all go like we did last time?"

"I doubt it," my father answered for me. "We've got to get the house painted while we've got a day or two free of fooling with crops."

"Oh, Frank, you old stick-in-the-mud," Aunt Ida said. "We'll just all get busy first thing in the morning and get it done. That way we'll save you at least a day and you can go fishing and have your work done both! What d'ya think of that?"

"Well," Dad said, hesitantly, "I guess if I could get my neighbor across the way to check the water for me, I might consider it. We'll see."

"Do it, Frank," Momma said, encouragingly. "You work too hard. You've hardly had a free day all summer long. I'll stay here with Pa and you can just go with your folks and take the kids with you so they can visit their cousins."

The Oakleys unpacked the rattletrap truck in no time and had a fire going for supper. With all their offhand ways, they seemed to incorporate a system of sorts. Aunt Ida whipped up pancake batter while Sylvan Oakley made the fire. The older boys arranged bedrolls, and Audra set the table my father had made out of a couple of Grandpa's sawhorses and some scrap lumber. I helped her.

All the while this was going on, Sylvan Oakley strung together the most amazing and interesting stories about his life I had ever heard. He'd done everything. His long list of adventures made our ordinary way of life pale by comparison. It was amazing to hear how close he had come to all sorts of big-time successful enterprises—how often he had missed fame by no more, as he contended, than a thread.

My father listened intently, his mouth rather grim, I thought. He did not enter into the conversation, but Sylvan Oakley seemed to take that contingency in his stride.

"Well, Frank," he said at last, "I have the inside track on an investment proposition that could make us all rich overnight."

"Really," my father replied.

"You bet. And not much of an investment, either."

"I think I'll pass it by," Dad said. "I can't afford to take risks right now. The new room has eaten up all my savings. Anyway, I've never been much of a gambler. Don't believe in it."

"Well, think about it," Sylvan Oakley urged. "Chance of a lifetime. No risk to it whatsoever."

"Your supper smells mighty good," my father observed, quite drastically changing the subject, I thought. "Nobody cooks like Ida," he said, reaching down and pinching my bare toe. "Not even Louise."

Sylvan Oakley knew how to conduct a fishing trip. After we'd painted the new room inside and out he planned the whole thing, and even had my father enthused. Sylvan Oakley was a lot of fun to be around; there were no two ways about it. That's what my mother said. My father replied, "Whatever you say, Louise."

"Well, what if he does exaggerate? Everyone has their faults," my mother answered. "What if he doesn't worry enough about the future? He certainly knows how to savor the moment at hand."

My father gathered his fishing tackle together.

"Wouldn't you say so, Frank?"

"Have you seen my sinkers, Louise?" my father answered.

But despite his wariness, Dad had a whopping time fishing with Sylvan Oakley on our overnight camping adventure.

"Just look at those two," Aunt Ida said. "Don't they remind you of a couple of kids?"

They did not, but I nodded my head anyway.

"I sure do like to see my two favorite men enjoying themselves like this," she continued. "We're just going to have to make it a point to get together more often."

I loved Aunt Ida; she was so comfortable to be around. Nothing seemed to bother her much. Her whole family was the same way. She was right about wanting us to get together more. I had been having loads of fun playing with Audra. We could get our faces dirty and splash mud on our legs and nobody made us comb our hair. We cooked over a smoky old fire and did exactly as we pleased. But somewhere along the line, around the middle of the second day, I noticed that Sylvan Oakley's stories lost some of their enchantment.

We hated to go home, but the Oakleys had to get back to Salt Lake. They camped one more night in our yard, and I got to camp out with them. Audra and I lay out between two old quilts and looked at the stars.

"Would you like to be my pen pal?" I asked. "My other cousin is a pen pal of mine."

"Sure," Audra said. "What do pen pals do?"

"They write letters all winter and then visit each other in the summertime," I said. "You'll have to write down your address for me on a piece of paper."

"That sounds fun," Audra said.

Soon she was asleep. All the Oakleys were asleep in our front yard. I lay awake, watching the stars and thinking about how different my father's world was from Sylvan Oakley's—wondering if there was a place one might inhabit somewhere between the two of them.

In the morning, bright and early, the Oakleys drove off, their beat-up old truck leaving a cloud of dust behind. I wrote several letters to Audra and eagerly ran out to the mail box every day, but she never did answer. One morning, though, a letter addressed to me did show up. It was written in Peggy's familiar hand—neat, round letters with tiny circles dotting the *i*'s. It began, as our letters always did, "Dear Nola: How are you? I am fine."

Kent Williamson wanted to be baptized. He was sure that was what he wanted and, he said, there was no use waiting around. This request brought his entire dilemma into such sharp focus that it could no longer be neglected.

"Clay, we've got to decide, and decide now," my father said. "It's not fair to the boy or ourselves to let it go any longer."

"I'm getting married next month, Frank," Clayton Hibbard answered. "And that's about all a man can handle at one time, don't you think?"

"Has nothing to do with the boy, Clay, your getting married. If you can't take him, we'll have to canvass the ward and see who might. Or turn him back. Better to be honest with him than string him along this way."

Mr. Hibbard stared at his hat rim as he turned it around and around. Finally he looked up at my father. "Give me until Monday, Frank. I'll talk to Glinnis. But I'm not sure it will get me anywhere."

"Want me to ask Lillian Brownstone? She's crazy to get that boy, seeing she's never had a child of her own."

"No! You're fooling, Frank!"

"Don't laugh, Clay; it's the truth. She's been running Louise ragged trying to enlist her in the cause. Seems she's taken a real liking to the kid."

"I can't see her taking a boy in to raise after all these years, can you? Especially as ornery as she is," Mr. Hibbard retorted. "If she wasn't gettin' so old, or even if Loren was still alive— but I sure don't think she's the one to adopt him."

"Doesn't seem a likely candidate, Clay, but I expect he might rather stay there than go back where he was."

"Oh, boy!" Clayton Hibbard sighed, pushing the kitchen chair back and rising to his feet. "I'll get back to you by Monday, like I said."

Grandpa had a few odds and ends to take care of before he went back to Red Rock for good. He was tired, but pleased with the results of his labor.

"What d'ye think, lass, of yer new room?" he asked.

"It's the best room in the whole world, Grandpa," I said. "I just love the big window—it lets you see the sun come up in the morning."

My grandfather's face flushed with pleasure. "Well, I did me best. I think it'll do."

That was the closest Grandpa ever came to bragging. If he realized he'd done a fantastic job, he'd say it would do.

"Are you really going home, Grandpa?" I asked. Even though I knew he had to, and that he belonged to the bigger family, he had made a spot in our own for himself, one that no one else could fill.

"Yep, I need to be goin' on home now. Your Uncle Rob has been doing his best to get his own household going and tend to mine too. And I worry about your grandma all alone there, day and night."

"I sure do hate to see you go, Pa," my mother said. She and Grandpa were so much alike that they could have been twins if they were the same age. "I worry about Ma, though, too."

She tucked a long strand of my hair into my braid. "We'll get used to it in a few days," she said to me.

"Tell ye what; we'll have one of those games of checkers, shall we?"

I got out the board. I'd become quite proficient at the game, practicing all summer with Grandpa. I had gotten so good that I was able to teach Jack to play. This I did at Grandpa's suggestion so as not to be without an opponent.

We placed our men on the board and began to play. I was still trying to beat Grandpa at just one game before he went back to Red Rock, and I put into my strategy every ounce of concentration I could muster.

Grandpa jumped one of my men, just as I'd intended for him to do. I jumped his in return. He hesitated longer than usual, and then did a really strange thing. He jumped one of his own checkers—sideways instead of diagonally.

I looked up. A peculiar expression was on his face. He removed the checker from the board and stared at it with embarrassment.

"This isn't a chess piece, is it?" he asked.

I didn't know what to say. Finally, I answered, "No, Grandpa, it isn't, but it doesn't matter. I don't care."

But Grandpa wasn't paying attention. He was staring off into thin air. I just sat there too, with my finger on one of my kings. Then he said something that wasn't in the least related to our checker game.

"I think I'll ride on up to Newcastle this afternoon."

I felt as though I were frozen to the chair, but I managed to finally ask, "Should we finish our checker game, Grandpa?"

He didn't answer my question. Suddenly, he stood up, knocking some of the checkers off the table with his hand. Then he walked slowly and unsteadily out into the vegetable garden.

I started looking for my mother. She'd left the house a few minutes before without saying where she was going. I scouted around the yard, keeping one eye on my grandfather, who was standing forlornly in the middle of the squash patch.

As I rounded the corner of the house I saw my mother taking clothes off the line. I ran up to her.

"Momma," I said, "something's gone wrong with Grandpa."

She let go of the clothes and they tumbled into the basket. "What's wrong with him?"

"I don't know. All of a sudden he just started using all the wrong checkers and talking about going to Newcastle."

"Where is he?" She had gone as white as the towels she had been unfastening from the line. She took me by the arm and began half-dragging me along, with a distracted, frightening strength.

"Out in the squashes," I said.

She let go of my arm and began to walk as fast as her condition would allow.

"Go up to the headgate and get your father," she said in a low, wooden sort of voice. "Tell him to hurry as fast as he can."

I ran as rapidly as I could through the wheat, not even caring whether I trampled it all down. I could see my father way up at the end of the field, walking toward me with a shovel over his shoulder. I kept on going as fast as I could until I was all out of breath. My father saw me and began to walk faster. I started to yell at him.

"Dad," I hollered, "Dad! Hurry!"

He dropped the shovel right on the spot and broke into a run. The only time I had ever seen him run before was when our cow had gotten loose. I waited until he got pretty close, and then I turned around and started running ahead of him back toward the house.

Chapter

8

Doc Powell put his tiny flashlight and his stethoscope back in his black bag and then leaned forward in his chair, his hands clenched between his knees. He looked my grandfather right in the eye.

"Mr. O'Toole," he said, "it appears that you've had a slight stroke—maybe more than one."

"What exactly do you mean by that, Doctor?" my mother snapped, almost as if the doctor had caused it.

Doc Powell paused for quite a while and then said to her in a much friendlier voice than hers, "Nothing exact about it, Louise. We can't ever tell what small strokes might or might not lead to. I'm not going to soft-pedal this just to make you feel better. I can say that it's nothing to take lightly."

He turned once more toward my grandfather.

"Mr. O'Toole, you probably have a physician of your own someplace nearer Red Rock, don't you?"

My grandfather nodded, his eyes full of terror.

"Could you give me his name, and tell me what town his office is in?"

"Name's Browning."

"Oh, yes, Phil Browning over in Pinto Valley. He the one you mean?"

Grandpa nodded again. Doc Powell took his silver watch out of his vest pocket.

"Let's see, it's already past office hours . . . Do you feel up to riding to your home tonight? If you don't we could wait until tomorrow, but I really would like to see you get with your own physician; he knows more about you than I do, and besides, you two are probably pretty good friends by now."

Doc Powell's quiet manner and smile apparently reassured my grandfather to the point that he could muster a weak smile in return and nod in agreement.

"Do you have a telephone here?" Doc asked my father.

"No, we haven't got around to that yet, Doc."

He turned back to my mother. "Do you have a way to get him home comfortably?"

"Well, yes. I could drive him, or I could call his neighbors and have them get hold of my brother Rob. I'd go along, of course."

Doc Powell sat down near Grandpa again. "That seems best to me, doesn't it to you, Mr. O'Toole—having your son come for you? That way there would be an extra person besides the driver in case you needed anything."

"Yes, lad," Grandpa said, trembling. "I'd like to be in me own house with me missus."

"We'll see that you get there, then. Tell you what I'm going to do. Even though it's getting a bit late, I'm going right straight home and call Dr. Browning and tell him all I know. That way, when he comes to see you he'll already know what's happened. He might want to take a look at you tonight, so don't be surprised if you see a strange car drive up in front of your place."

My grandfather nodded, his expression oddly childlike.

"I want you to take some drinking water along, Mr. O'Toole, and have a couple of sips every now and then. If you get tired or hot, tell your daughter, and she'll stop the car and see that you get plenty of fresh air. Does that sound all right?"

My mother stood rigidly through all this, never taking her eyes off the doctor's face.

"Now, Louise—make sure it's a peaceful trip. Don't let him get too tired. He's going to have to get plenty of rest for the next few weeks."

Momma nodded. "I'll take good care of him. Don't worry."

"Good. Now all of you try not to get excited. I know that's easier said than done, but it's mighty important, believe me. Especially you, Mr. O'Toole. Try to think of pleasant things. It won't be easy, but I believe you can do it. Now, is there someplace I can take you to make your telephone call, Louise? Be glad to do it and bring you on back home again."

When my mother and the doctor had gone, Dad sat down beside the couch where my grandfather lay and awkwardly but gently patted his hand.

"Patrick," he said, "I suspect everything will be all right."

"Think so, do ye, Frank, lad?" my grandfather replied, imploringly.

"Why, sure, Pat. You've always been a tough old nut. It'll take more than a little setback like this to bother a chap like you any. You're bound to come out of this just fine."

"There's one thing, Frank; I'd like to be administered to. Could ye arrange to get someone in to help ye give me a blessing?"

"I should've thought of that myself before this, Patrick," my father answered. "Nola, you might have a hard time running Clay down—I believe he's working his other place today. Hurry on over to Alvin Taylor's, will you? And tell

Ruth you'll tend her kids while she gets hold of Alvin."

I ran down the road to the Taylors' place. We were lucky. Mr. Taylor was working right by the fence, so I could give him the message by myself. He stopped briefly by the house to tell Mrs. Taylor where he was going.

He didn't own a car, so he jumped bareback on his horse and headed down the road, leaving me to get home on my own.

By the time I got back, the blessing was over.

"How do you feel, Grandpa?" I asked.

"Better, lass," he answered. "Ah, yes, lass, much better now."

The terrible fear had gone out of his eyes. They even twinkled a little, like they used to, and his mouth broke into a faint smile.

With all that had been going on, we'd forgotten to eat. My father realized this as dusk began to settle in. He opened the refrigerator, looked in, and shut it again.

"Guess your mother didn't get supper ready," he said. "What'll it be? I'll give you your choice: bread and milk or fried eggs and toast."

We opted for bread and milk. It was not a supper we were unaccustomed to eating at the end of busy summer days. I went out into the garden and pulled up some of the last of the radishes and cleaned them while Jack set the table and Billy emptied the wash basin. My father sliced thick, crooked slabs of cheese and plunked them unceremoniously on a plate.

"You see?" he said, smiling at me as if I had questioned his ability. "We got us a good supper ready all by ourselves. We're gonna do just fine."

But he had forgotten about the beans. I wished I had too, but that was impossible, because I'd seen Momma pause in the midst of her hurried packing and say to herself, "It's all my fault; I should never have let him build that room. He's too old. No matter what he said, I knew he wasn't up to it!"

Then, after she had packed a few more things and fastened the latch on her suitcase, she'd looked out of the window and whispered, "Oh, no! The beans!"

Not only did I hear the words but I knew the interpretation. My mother's pole beans were the pride and joy of her summer. The beans from the year before hadn't done too well, so this spring Momma had determined to grow pole beans. She went out on the canal bank and cut down dozens of thick poles. She placed them deep in the ground and tied them together. She planted the beans and fertilized them and watered them well. She did it all with delight. Now they were next to ready—maybe ready right this minute, for all I knew. A hundred quarts at least; in her own words. Worst of all, she had put me in charge.

"Well, Nola, I guess you're going to have to be the mother for a few days around here. It can't be helped. You'll just have to take my place. I'm taking Billy with me, but I want you to keep an eye on Jack. Don't let him anywhere near the canal. Did you hear that, Jack? If you even *look* like you might *think* about going *near* that canal, I'm giving Nola permission to switch your legs with a willow; it's better than drowning. Nola, you mustn't switch him for anything else. Oh, if there were someone to leave you with—but they're all too busy in the fields and gardens this time of year, and I'm afraid Jack and Billy together might make too much of a ruckus and make Pa nervous!"

"We'll get by, Louise," my father had said, reassuringly. "There's not a thing you do around here can't be done by the three of us if we make our minds up to it."

I had made my mind up to it. I had made my mind up to neither switching Jack's legs nor letting him drown in the canal. Everywhere I went, Jack went with me. If I swept the floor, Jack held the dustpan. If I made beds, Jack plumped the pillows. After a while he got pretty tired of it, and then I would placate him by putting two kitchen chairs together and reading him stories while he ate bread and jam. I wouldn't let him go outside alone for one minute to play a solitary game of marbles. And I was making plans to do something about those beans, too.

Jack and Kent Williamson were way up on the hill ahead of me. I was trying to catch up with them, but I kept slipping and sliding on the pole beans. Whenever I tried to move my arms and legs, they simply wouldn't respond. At the top of the hill was a cliff. Kent Williamson and Jack were getting closer and closer to the ridge, where they would surely fall two or three miles into the water and be goners for certain. Behind me I could hear my father calling, "Nola, Nola."

"Nola. What in tarnation's going on here?"

Dad was shaking my shoulder. It was pitch dark. For a few moments I didn't know where I was; then I realized I was in the middle of the kitchen floor.

"I don't know."

"Well, you're walking and talking in your sleep. I couldn't make out what you were saying, but you scared me about to death."

My father switched the light on.

"You sick?"

"No. Just having a bad dream."

"Have you ever walked in your sleep before that you know of?" He looked anxious.

"No, I never have. I don't have bad dreams very often."

"Well, then, I guess we can go back to bed."

"Dad, do you think Jack's all right?"

"Why, sure he's all right."

"Would you go up and check to make sure?"

"He's fine," my father said, "but if it'll make you feel any better I'll check."

The house was so empty without Momma and Grandpa that I could almost hear it echoing, especially with Dad up in the attic. I was glad when he came back down and told me Jack was perfectly okay.

"You go on back to bed, now," he said. "I've got to get some sleep. We're starting the threshing tomorrow, bright and early."

"Daddy?" I slipped—I hadn't called him Daddy for about a year—"Would you get me up when you wake up?"

"Sure you want to get up that early? No real reason for you to."

"Yes. And Dad, do you care if I leave the light on just this once?"

"Nah, go ahead," he answered. "Seems kind of funny around here without your mother, doesn't it?"

Things were falling into place just perfectly. My father would be eating dinner at the Hall's place. He'd asked Glinnis Quince to look in on me, but she was a teacher and didn't understand a thing about gardening, so I could probably keep her fooled.

Dad had called me at the crack of dawn, as he'd promised, and I'd gotten Jack up and fixed milk toast for him and Dad and myself. The minute Dad left, Jack and I took off for the store. It was seven o'clock, and I figured we'd get there right after they opened at seven-thirty.

It was wonderful to be out on the road that time of morning, with everything so dewy and fresh and still cool. We hurried right along.

"What do we have to go to the store first thing in the morning for?" Jack asked.

"You'll see."

It paid not to tell Jack more than you needed to. He couldn't keep his mouth shut.

Lillian Brownstone would have to be in the store this particular morning, of all times! I'd been hoping against hope she wouldn't be. But I wasn't going to let her stop me.

"What'll you have this early in the morning?" Charlie asked.

"Oh, about nine boxes of Mason Jar lids," I said.

"Sounds like your ma is fixin' to do a bunch of canning," Lillian said. "What's she putting up? Must be beans."

"Yes, it's beans, all right," I answered.

"But Momma's not putting them up," Jack said. "She's at my Grandpa's place."

"Well, just who's canning, then, I'd like to know?"

Jack looked at me, questioningly.

"I am," I said, taking out of my pocket the grocery money Momma had left with me.

"You ain't gonna do no such a thing!" Lillian said.

"Yes I am," I said. "I've helped Momma before. I'm just not sure how I'm going to get the boiler on top of the stove, but I'll figure it out."

"Did you hear that, Charlie? Are you listenin' to this?" Lillian said.

"Yeah, but I don't believe it," Charlie said.

"Well, you can just start believing it," I said. "Because my grandpa had a stroke and my mother thinks it's all her fault because she let him build a bedroom for me. And on top of that, her beans are just going to get big and bulgy and fall right down on the ground. It isn't fair."

Partway through this speech I felt unexpected tears sting my eyelids.

"And I suppose it'll just tickle your ma pink to come home and find out you've gone and scalded yourself to death!"

"There's something to what Lillian says," Charlie concurred. "I don't think I should sell you those lids until I talk to your dad."

"My mother gave me this money. And my dad says we can do whatever she does. How much do they cost?"

"Two for a quarter," Charlie said.

"Then give me a dollar and a quarter's worth," I demanded.

The smart thing to do, I decided, was to start with the things I personally had done before. So I got out a whole lot of quart jars and ran my finger around the rims to check for chips. I set a couple of chipped bottles to one side.

I guessed the next step would be to gather the produce, so I got the biggest pans I could find and, with Jack to help, headed out to the bean poles. We'd hardly got the bottoms of the pans covered when Glinnis Quince came by. She insisted on helping, even though I told her I could do it by myself. I was glad, even though, being a town person, she didn't know beans about beans, I supposed. But you never knew for sure, so I asked her.

"No, as a matter of fact I've never canned beans, but I've picked a few in my time."

"Do you know how to keep from tearing the vines off the poles?" I asked.

"I'll watch, and do it the way you do," she answered. She was mighty slow, so I got my mother's big dripper pan and showed her how to snap the ends off. I left her there and went into the house to start washing bottles. I was putting off figuring out the hard part, but with Miss Quince there I was sure it would somehow be easier.

Suddenly there was a banging on the door that would raise the dead. I hurried to answer. There, of all people, stood Lillian Brownstone holding a big boiler.

"If it's beans you want, it's beans you're gonna get!" she said. "Let's get a move on, we ain't got all day."

Then she barged right in, sort of pushing me to one side as if I were a housefly. But the way she banged that boiler against the kitchen floor, I could tell she knew what she was doing. The gesture had the loud ring of authority to it even before the words that followed.

"Now, I'm the boss here. If we're gonna put up your ma's beans and do it right without nobody ending up in the hospital or graveyard, you'd better mind every word I say. Who's that out in your garden?"

"It's that Miss Quince—the woman who's going to marry Mr. Hibbard."

"What's she doin' here?"

"My dad asked her to look in on us and she's trying to help. I've got her snapping bean ends."

"Well, that's a good place for her—teach 'er that real work ain't like sittin' around a school room all day, twiddling her thumbs."

I had thought the very same thing until Lillian Brownstone put it into words, but now I sprang to Miss Quince's defense.

"She's a nice lady," I said. "Really nice."

"Humph!" said Lillian Brownstone. "Better than nothin', I suppose. About time that old bachelor started living like a regular human. Well, you just get yourself over to them girls' place you run around with—that Simpson girl and—what's her name? That new one."

"Grace Jacobson."

"Yeah, her. Now go tell their mas we need help worse'n they do, and don't you come back without 'em, hear?"

I didn't come back without them, though I was surprised at how quickly their mothers agreed to Lillian Brownstone's blueprint. The whole thing seemed to hinge on Grandpa's illness. There was something disturbing about this; it must mean that the situation was worse than I had thought. But in my mind I kept going back to the way my father had told Grandpa it was just a little setback. I shrugged it off, glad to have this small army of helpers gathering in behalf of the beans.

"You!" Mrs. Brownstone announced, pointing at Beverly. "You stay in here and bottle-wash. You got little hands to reach in the jars with. And don't go leaving the corners."

She had done an amazing amount of organizing in the short time I'd been gone. She stood facing us, her hands on her hips.

"And you other three go on out with that school teacher. And be sure not to pick the patch clean. Leave the little ones so's they'll be there for the next picking."

"She's just the bossiest old woman I ever saw!" Beverly Simpson said, as I left her and took off for the bean patch. "If it wasn't for you, I wouldn't pick one single bean."

We hurried from vine to vine, trying to make the most of our opportunity. After an hour or so had passed, Miss Quince raised her hand, studied it, and murmured, "Oh dear—look at what's happened. What do you think I should do?"

The tips of a couple of her fingers were bleeding.

"I don't know; maybe we'd better go in and ask Mrs. Brownstone," I answered. There really was something nice about having a boss.

"She's someone I've never met before," Miss Quince said, "so I hope you'll introduce me."

Although that prospect was frightening—I had never before made an introduction—I followed her into the kitchen and did the best I knew how.

"Well, glad to make your acquaintance," Lillian Brownstone said, smiling expansively and revealing a brand new side of her personality. She wiped her hands on the front of her apron and extended one of them. Miss Quince, flustered, offered her delicate but injured hand in return.

"Glory!" Lillian exclaimed. "What's happened to your fingers?"

"It seems I'm not used enough to this kind of work. I'm sorry. Do you think I should go on, or is there something else I could do?"

"I've heard say you're a mighty fine cook," Mrs. Brownstone said. "Heard your biscuits are so light they purt' near float right off a plate."

I couldn't believe my ears. Hearing a compliment come out of Lillian Brownstone was like seeing a river of dust.

"Well . . . thank you very much."

"So how'd you like to just cook up a mess of stew or something else easy for this crew. I'll get some money out of my purse."

"No, Mrs. Brownstone," I interjected, "my dad wouldn't like that. Momma left some grocery money. Let me get it."

"Oh, please," Miss Quince answered, shaking her head. "That's not necessary. I have plenty of food, and will be glad to prepare a meal. It's the least I can do."

"My dad will be mad at me, Miss Quince. It's real nice of you to offer to cook supper. But we'll have to pay for the groceries."

Miss Quince stood there vacillating uneasily.

"Frank Borden brung his kids up right, Miss Quince," Lillian said. "At least in one respect. Let 'er give you the money. Usually folks don't eat supper around here till eight or nine o'clock in the summer, so take your time."

Lillian watched the school teacher walk out and get into her car. She shook her head. "How's a woman who can't snap beans without bleeding gonna deal with that scallywag of a Norman Hibbard?" she said. "Too bad he ain't more like that Kent Williamson. Now, there's a boy for you!"

My father came in, all covered with wheat dust from threshing, at the same time Miss Quince drove up with our supper. He took some of the food from her and they talked for a minute or two before he came inside.

"Well, Frank," Lillian Brownstone said, beaming, as he came into the kitchen, "I'll have you know we done thirty-two quarts of beans; in one little day."

My father shook his head, smiling. "All I have to say, Lillian, is that you sure did save our bacon. I figured we might as well just write those beans off."

Lillian Brownstone looked sideways at me. She was going to tell Dad what happened in the store; I could feel it coming. Right on the heels of the trouble I'd had the first of summer over Kent Williamson and his camping.

"Well, I heard tell from *somebody* that your wife's pa was took sick, so I thought to myself, 'Bet Louise's beans must be about ready, too.' So I just moseyed on over, and sure enough they was."

She gave me a smirky sort of a grin, adding, "I'll come back in four, five days, after I finish putting up my own, and do thirty-two more if Louise ain't back yet."

"Well, I sure do thank you kindly, Lillian," my father replied. "Don't know how I'll ever pay you back, but there's sure to be something I can do for you some day."

"That's okay, Frank," she said, as she walked out of the door.

"She sure is bossy!" Jack said, when she'd gone.

"Oh, her bark's worse than her bite," Dad answered. "She's a good soul."

After we'd eaten Miss Quince's stew and angel food cake I saw to it that the boys got to bed, then went in to the front room, where my father was reading.

"Dad, when is Momma coming home?" I asked.

"Not for a while," he said. "Glinnis Quince stopped at the store just before she brought our supper out. They had just had a telephone call from your mother. Your grandpa hasn't got any better."

He put his paper down. "In fact, he's some worse. No telling when she'll be back."

I missed my mother. You could put Miss Quince and Mrs. Brownstone together and times them by ten and they still wouldn't take my mother's place. Maybe that was the way Norman Hibbard felt.

"I know it's late," I said to Dad, "but I wonder if we couldn't play just one game of checkers."

A look of surprise crossed his face.

"Why, I think we could manage to find time for one game," he said.

I got the checkers and board down from their place on top of the cupboard and laid them all out neatly, squaring the board off to the table top exactly, straight as a string, the way Grandpa always did.

"And don't let me beat you anymore," I said. "I'll never learn to be a champion that way."

Chapter

9

Kent Williamson's lamb was still following him, even though it was getting to be half grown. At first he'd made a leash for it, but he never had to use it, so when it started tightening on Rapscallion's neck as the lamb grew, Kent whittled through the leather strap and decided to let him go loose like the other sheep. Rapscallion, however, stayed at his heels. He even played baseball with us.

We were allowed to throw together a makeshift baseball diamond, now that our wheat was harvested. It was close to the house, but far enough back that there was little danger of breaking a window. The bases consisted of gunny sacks filled with sand from the canal bank. Our two teams, which were freshly chosen each day by drawing straws, were sparse, having three members each. But at least that gave each team a pitcher, a catcher, and a fielder, which was better than it had been before Kent and Grace came around. Rapscallion was our cheerleader.

"Get back, sheep!" Kent said, irritably. "Durn old sheep just about cost me my job."

"Which job?" Grace asked. Kent had jobs of some sort with half the town.

"Weeding Mrs. Brownstone's petunias," he answered. "Rapscallion started eating them when my back was turned. Mrs. Brownstone didn't like it one bit, and said I'd have to keep him penned up from now on if I want to work for her."

"Lucky you, if you get fired," Beverly said. "I'd as leave work for a slave driver."

"Oh, she's been nice enough," Kent said. "Sewed me three new shirts for school, and wouldn't take a dime for them."

"You'll just have to pen him up, then," I said, "when you go weed her petunias." I had a different view of Lillian Brownstone since she'd got me out of my scrape without tattling.

"Oh, well, the summer's about over, anyway," Kent said. "Guess I'll be back in school pretty soon. Some school. There's a big conference going on right now about me, I guess."

Norman was out playing field, or Kent wouldn't have been telling us. We all knew that Norman's father was a top contender. So far, we hadn't heard Norman's opinion. Maybe he wanted to go back to things the way they were, or at least as close as he could get considering he would soon have a new mother.

"Think if they send you back you'll run away instead?" I asked.

"Nah," he answered. "That's just kid stuff. You can't hide out from people, I found that out. Just makes things worse. No, if there's no place for me here, I'll go back and make the best of it."

Even though it had only been a little over two months,

Kent seemed to have grown a lot older. His field work had made him tanned and more muscular. Norman had grown this summer, too. Kent had spoken of kid stuff. There was something to what he said; they didn't seem quite like kids anymore, either of them.

"Well, if you do go back we'll stop and get you every Saturday that we get to go to a picture show," Beverly said. "I'll save my baby-sitting money."

"Me too," Grace said. "I'll buy you some popcorn."

That seemed to take care of the theater business. I offered lamely, "I'll make fudge."

We played ball, but our hearts weren't in it. We had just heard something on the radio we hoped was a mistake. They had said that hundreds of Jews had been killed near the border between Germany and Russia. Surely, it couldn't be true.

Lillian Brownstone had canned another thirty-two quarts of beans and was starting to take a look at the corn patch. However, Glinnis Quince had alerted the Relief Society, who had come over one at a time taking bushel baskets full of corn and returning bottles filled with golden, gleaming kernels, and most often supper to boot. The only problem left was to find a tactful way to get them to leave enough for table use. So Lillian scoured the cucumber patch and made pickles. She also did a few quarts of Momma's tomatoes, open kettle. Still, Momma hadn't come home. But my father said that it wouldn't be long. She missed us and was looking for a hired woman to stay with Grandma so she could leave for a few days, at least.

Now that the wheat was harvested Dad had more time to take care of things around the place, so my summer was getting to be more normal. The wheat had brought such a good price that my father took us to town one day and let us buy a few ready-made clothes for school, so Momma wouldn't have to worry about that.

But I was still having trouble sleeping. Dad had moved my bed into the new room and I hadn't yet gotten used to being all alone. One night, late, after I had drifted off to sleep, I was awakened by the voices of my father and Clayton Hibbard.

"I'll tell you, Frank, I decided to call his bluff."

"In what way?"

"Well, I said, 'Norman, looks like you don't want a mother very much. Maybe you like things the way they were. Maybe I'd ought to call it off and then take Kent back on up to the school, and it'll just be the two of us again. You think about it, and let me know.' "

My heart almost stopped beating.

"That was a devil of a risk, Clay. What if he'd agreed?"

"Don't even like to think about it, Frank. Point is, before long he came wandering out to the field and says, 'Pa, I been thinkin'. Only seems fair that if you get a wife I should get a brother out of it.' "

"He did?"

"Yeah. Just like that. After he'd got really pondering on it, guess he remembered that it got pretty lonesome around here with just us two old codgers. Well, let's face it, Frank—he was kind of a spoiled kid. He's got lots better since the Williamson boy moved in."

I could never remember a time when I'd been happier. The Hibbards were going to adopt Kent!

"Have you told the boy yet?"

"Yes, we have."

"What does Glinnis think of all this; inheriting two ready-made boys?"

"Tickled to death, Frank. You know, Glinnis is a few years older than I am. It's hard to know whether we'll have time for too many of our own. She's wanted a family for a lot of years."

I thought about Lillian Brownstone, who'd never had

children of her own. She'd be disappointed. I hoped not too much. Maybe Kent would pen up Rapscallion and still weed her petunias. I'd suggest it to him.

"What I came about, other than to give you the good news, Frank, is to ask your advice on a couple of matters that pertain to this."

"Why, sure. If I can help."

"Now, I've got in touch with the boy's grandmother, and she is trying to reach the boy's father. Think I should get me a lawyer or something? What I'm afraid of is the man may have second thoughts."

It didn't seem to me that a man who would abandon his child should have a right to second thoughts. But there were a lot of things I just didn't understand. My experience with Mrs. Brownstone had brought me to a different level of realization than I'd previously had about the complexities of life.

"Let me ask you this, Clay," my father said. "How are you fixed for money?"

"That's not a problem," Mr. Hibbard said.

"Then I think you've got something there. A lawyer could advise you how to go about it, too. You'll want it to be legal, so no bugaboo can come back on you from out of the blue. Have you called the reform school?"

"Yes, I have. They're willing to let me get Kent enrolled in school here; they'll go that far."

"I think you're right on the mark, Clay. If I were you I'd go ahead and line me up a lawyer, and then just wait and see what happens."

"Well, thanks for your time, Frank. I know it's late, but I felt like I wanted to talk it over with somebody right now."

"Glad you did, Clay."

I stayed awake for another hour at least, thinking back to the day we'd run into Kent Williamson down by the railroad tracks, of his camping place, of all the days the whole bunch of us had gone swimming in the canal. He was going to be our neighbor. The Hibbards were going to be a whole different family. I thought about Norman's mother. I'd never even seen her in person, only a faded photograph they kept on their living room wall. Would Mr. Hibbard take her picture down now, and if so, what would he do with it?

I wanted Momma to come home that minute. I missed her something awful, and I missed my little brother, Billy, too.

I spent a couple of evenings making a handkerchief for Lillian Brownstone out of a square of soft white cotton material I confiscated from my mother's scraps. I sewed some fine white lace around the edge and left the hallmark of my painstaking, if questionable, embroidery in one corner; purple lilacs, my favorite. This I wrapped in some white tissue paper left over from Christmas and tied it with a scrap of purple ribbon.

When she first came in with her pint jars of mustard pickles, I didn't have the courage to present it to her. I'd been down in the field taking a jar full of fresh, cold drinking water to my father and had just gotten out the cookbook to start on supper.

"I hope you ain't going in over your head on what you're cooking," Mrs. Brownstone said. "Don't be biting off more than you can chew."

"I won't," I said. "I'm only going to use up the left-over rice for a rice pudding."

"That sounds safe enough, I guess. Got everything you need?"

"Nearly," I said. "We're all out of raisins, but I don't think that will matter, do you?"

"I don't know, rice pudding without raisins . . . You don't happen to have a can of pineapple?"

"No," I said. "We can't afford that."

"You've been doin' an awful good job of housekeeping since your mother's been gone," she said. "Keeping this place as neat as a pin, and cooking, too."

"It isn't hard," I said, "if you read the recipe and don't forget and leave something important out." I didn't admit it, but my first experiment had been a cake and I'd forgotten to put in the baking powder.

There was one cookie left from the last batch the Relief Society had brought around, so I served it to Mrs. Brownstone with a glass of milk. While she was eating, I slipped into my bedroom and got her present.

"Well, land, who's this for? Me?"

Her face flushed with undeniable pleasure. She unwrapped it gently. "Why, it's just absolutely beautiful," she said. "This here community is really raising some good youngsters. Even that Norman Hibbard is starting to act half-way civilized. And that Kent Williamson—there's a boy I could raise, myself."

I took a deep breath. She had to know sometime. Somebody had to tell her.

"I guess the Hibbards are going to adopt him," I said. "You know Mr. Hibbard's getting married in a couple of weeks."

A brief expression of pain flitted over her face but was almost instantly replaced by a jovial grin. "Do tell! Ain't that nice; glad they won't be taking him back to the reform school."

She tucked the handkerchief into the waistband of her front-apron. "Well, I can't sit here all day. I'm goin' out to see if there's anything else needs takin' care of in your ma's garden."

"Want me to help?" I asked.

"No. You just go on with fixin' your meal. I'll stop back in before I go."

After I'd beaten the eggs and measured the milk, sugar, vanilla, and salt and checked them twice, I walked over to the window and looked out into the garden. Mrs. Brownstone was bending over a row of carrots weeping into the handkerchief I had given her.

I ducked back from the window so she wouldn't see me, and proceeded to mix the ingredients of my rice pudding together. Before I was quite finished, she tapped on the door.

"Hold off on that pudding," she said, "I'm gonna bring back a few raisins. Rice pudding ain't no good without raisins."

If Kent Williamson knew that Lillian Brownstone had wanted to adopt him, he never mentioned it, and neither did I, especially the day of the celebration. He was much too ebullient. Mr. Hibbard waited until Saturday to throw a party for him so he could take the whole kit and caboodle of us, girls and boys, including Jack, up to the show house to see a matinee. Afterward we all went to the Purple Spur Café for chop suey. It was only the third time I could remember having eaten in a real restaurant, and I knew I was not alone. It took a really special occasion in Wind Valley for someone to splurge to that extent.

"I could hardly even pay attention to the show," Kent said, "I'm so keyed up."

"Well, you're all acting like a bunch of wild Indians," Mr. Hibbard said. "Better start settling down, or they'll kick us out of this place."

But for all his talk, Clayton Hibbard seemed as wild as the next one. And so did Norman.

By the time we got home it was almost dark. My father was frying a couple of eggs for his supper and asking us about the celebration when we heard a car door slam in front of the house.

Dad slid the pan over to the warming part of the stove, put the egg turner down, and went over to the screen door. I heard Charlie Branson's voice say, "Frank, could I speak to you outside here for a minute?"

What was Charlie doing here, anyway? He was supposed to be tending the store. I stayed right where I was. When someone asked your parent to talk with him somewhere else, I knew it meant they didn't want you listening. But I could see them—my father leaning against the gate post, Charlie Branson holding on to the open gate.

After a while, Charlie climbed in his car and drove away, but my father just kept standing there, his fingertips hooked into the back pocket of his overalls. Finally, he slowly turned and came back into the house, hesitating at the doorway.

"Don't you want your eggs, Daddy?" Jack asked.

"Come over here, Jack," my father said. "You too, Nola."

He walked us over to the couch and sat down between us, putting one of his large, rough hands on each of our shoulders. I didn't like the feel of things at all.

He sighed deeply. "There's something I need to tell you. You know Grandpa O'Toole was awfully sick. Well, he just got sicker and sicker; he couldn't get better."

"What do you mean, couldn't get better?" I asked angrily.

"Well—there's no way but to tell you straight out, I guess. Your grandpa died today."

Jack started to cry. I threw my father's hand off my shoulder and went over and knelt in front of Jack.

"You shouldn't have told Jack that," I said. "Charlie Branson must have got it wrong. He made a mistake, that's all."

My father looked at me in amazement. "What are you talking about? There's no mistake. Your grandpa had another stroke—a bad one this time. It took him."

How could my father be doing this?

"No. He just had a little setback. You said so, yourself. I heard you. You told him he'd be just fine. You said he was a tough old nut."

My father had put Jack, who was now sobbing, on his lap. He reached his hand out to me, but I backed away.

"Now, wait a minute. I can see how you'd have misunderstood. It was important that your grandpa stop being scared. I said I *thought* he'd be all right."

"You said he'd come out of it just fine!"

My father had his arms around Jack. I was standing all alone, feeling my father moving farther and farther away. He hadn't told the truth, and now he wanted to argue about it. And I still suspected he and Charlie Branson had just made that story up for no reason.

"You don't care," I said. "He's not your relation. You don't care at all!"

"Of course I care; he is my relation. And Patrick was a friend of mine, besides. A good friend."

Then I started noticing the eggs. They were just sitting there, going to waste. I noticed that the rug was crooked, and I walked over to straighten it. All my attention became riveted to silly details of how things were arranged in the house. My father was speaking, but everything he said sounded like the worst sort of foolishness.

"Your grandpa was an old man. It was his time. Everybody has to die when they get old. And you know our spirits don't die; when they leave our bodies they're happier than they've ever been."

I didn't want to hear one more word, so I turned on my heel and walked right out of the house. I walked down the road to the canal bridge. I climbed over the barbed wire fence and started down the canal bank. My father was calling my name over and over, but for the first time in my life I ignored him by refusing to answer. I kept right on going.

The fact that darkness was falling didn't bother me at all.

I sat down and watched the fading bits of light gleam on the ripples of water. The noise the ripples made sounded like an endless, quiet tune. As it became darker, the stars showed up, one by one, glistening and remote. Every few minutes my father would call again.

It grew cold. I sat shivering in the darkness, really alone for the first time in my life. Usually I only said my prayers when I got up in the morning and before I went to bed at night. But now I knelt on the dew-damp bank of the canal and said my prayers about Grandpa.

When I'd finished, the strangest thing happened. In the piercing chill of the evening I suddenly felt warm all over, as if somebody had wrapped me in a soft blanket. And I knew it must be my imagination or the sound of the light wind in the cottonwoods, but plain as day I heard from way far off, very far, the sound of Grandpa's bagpipes playing. There was no mistaking the sound. It was real. So real that I could even hear the words.

And should we die before our journey's through,
Happy day! All is well!

I started back toward the house. I hadn't gone far before I saw something in the path ahead of me, moving.

"Nola, is that you?"

"Yes, Daddy. I'm sorry I ran away. I should have answered."

He put his arm around my shoulder.

"It hurts bad, real bad, to lose a person you love," he said.

"I know he's in heaven, but he won't be here anymore."

"That's right. He's in paradise."

We walked in silence for a while. I could feel tears running down my cheeks.

"But I think he really is all right, Daddy, just like you said. He just had a little setback, didn't he?"

Chapter

10

Always, in late August, the weather's mood changed overnight. One day would be hot and silent and overripe, like someone getting cranky after too much of a good thing. But early the following morning the air that came through my cracked bedroom window would have an edge to it. A stray leaf here and there would fall into the lengthening shadows, a silent announcement of autumn's coming. It would have been a sad time if school hadn't started then.

Regardless of how we all complained, we were secretly glad to be back in the classroom. It gave us a chance to rub elbows with friends we only saw at church and a few we hadn't seen throughout the summer.

I had learned a valuable lesson several school grades back. It wasn't smart to make public your love for school and feelings of friendship toward teachers unless you wanted to be shunned by your peers. An extremely silly but accurate state of affairs.

Because of this, when Beverly Simpson asked, "Oh, school, again! Don't you just *hate* it?" I always said yes, I did. Hated it like all get-out. Kent Williamson had more self-assurance.

"I like school," he said. "I'd better; I'm going to be a science teacher."

He could get away with it, because he was the tallest person in the school other than the instructors. But there was another less easily definable reason. He had the quiet air of one who has reached maturity ahead of time. Any adult seeking a spokesman within our group would automatically be drawn to Kent and would pay no more attention to the rest of us than water dripping from a tap.

One of the best things about having Kent around was that now Norman had someone to walk to school with and was too ashamed to resume his previous childish behavior. He stopped throwing dirt clods at us and started acting almost harmless. Now that Kent Williamson and Grace Jacobson were a part of our little entourage, we separated in distinct groups—girls and boys. However, the boys fell behind just slightly, staying close enough to direct bantering remarks our way: "You've got mud all over your dress"—or some equally fatuous lie which, without exception, we pointedly disregarded.

This particular day we were in different groupings. Beverly and Grace were searching for samples for their leaf-collecting club. I had declined membership in this latest organization, being involved in more important endeavors. My skill at hemming diapers had prompted Momma to let me graduate to helping her sew tiny, sweet gowns of outing flannel for the new baby.

Norman and Jack were skipping rocks on the surface of the ditch. Kent Williamson fell into step with me and bluntly stated, "My real dad is coming to see me right after the wedding."

"I know," I said. "He's going to stay overnight at our house."

"At your house? How come?"

I floundered in silence for a tactful answer and finally said, "You know . . . he has to stay somewhere, and it would make him and the Hibbards both feel funny if he stayed over there."

I hadn't figured this out all by myself. It had come to me through my parents' conversations, from which I gleaned the sketchy information that legal matters beyond my understanding were going to have to be taken care of. I did know that Mr. Williamson needed to sign some papers.

"I guess it would, at that," Kent replied. His spirits were obviously pretty low. I hadn't seen him like this since the day he'd come from under the canvas tent in the rainstorm.

"You can visit him all you want at our place," I said. "I'll bet my dad wouldn't even care if you wanted to sleep on the floor. Or you could camp out with him in the yard—we'd put the quilts out like we did for the Oakleys, and you and your dad could catch up on things with nobody else getting in your way."

"Thanks. But I'll just have to see when the time comes."

I waited for more. I wanted him to tell me what it felt like to know you'd be seeing a father who hadn't bothered to get in touch with you for years. But he didn't, and it was the sort of thing you couldn't ask about.

"Yep," he said, after we had walked in silence for a time, "I'm going to be a science teacher. I'm going to get married and have about ten kids and take them fishin' every day all summer long. And in the winter time we'll build snowmen and find the longest hill in the country to go sledding down. That's what I'm going to do."

Mr. Hibbard and Miss Quince had decided to keep the wedding as low-key as possible so as not to ruffle Norman's feathers.

"Perfectly ridiculous!" my father said. "Letting a half-baked kid tyrannize them that way. Why, it's the silliest thing I ever heard tell of."

Momma agreed. That's why she planned a surprise reception for them while they were in Salt Lake getting married. My father thought she already had enough to do with the new baby coming.

"But I want to do something," Momma said. "Not just for the Hibbards, but for everybody who was so good to us while Pa was sick. I'll keep it simple. Just make a few cakes and a milk can full of grape punch. I promise I won't overdo."

"Well, it would be a shame to do nothing at all—Clay probably doesn't care one way or another, but Glinnis deserves some sort of celebration, all right," my father answered. "Maybe I'd better hire you some help."

"Nola will help me," Momma said. "And I can think of a few others around here to put to work, too."

"Well, be sure you don't try throwing that heavy milk can around. Let me at least get it cleaned up for you."

It was touching the way my father, naturally awkward when it came to household chores, was endeavoring to help my mother these days. It made me want to try harder, too. Our combined efforts gave me a new feeling of camaraderie with Dad.

"I will, Frank," my mother said. "Don't worry. It's just that Glinnis Quince has always taken a back seat. Somebody, for once, needs to put her in the spotlight. She'd never put herself there in a million years."

Momma turned from her job of cracking ice into pieces and said, "Norman, would you please put those chairs over under the weeping willow tree? And I'm going to make it your responsibility to see that nobody under twenty sits in them—we're short of seats, so these have to be saved for the older folks."

Norman stared at her defiantly.

"On second thought, Norman, sit down here a minute."

He continued to stare.

"I said, *sit down.*"

He sat down but did not alter his facial expression one iota. My mother, meeting and surpassing the ferociousness of his gaze, added, "Nola, get us each a glass of punch."

Because of all the cakes, I had a hard time getting to the milk can full of punch. Momma had tried to stop the Relief Society from baking so many, but to no avail.

I poured the punch, stuck a few pieces of ice in each glass, and set it in front of them.

"Now, Norman, we're going to talk turkey. It's about time somebody told you a few things you apparently are choosing to remain ignorant of. One of them is this: you've got no right sulking around this way, considering your dad's about the nicest person in Wind Valley, with Glinnis Quince running a close second."

Norman continued to glare.

"Your father has been married now for three days. There's nothing you can do about it," my mother continued, "except one thing. You can try to be happy for him. And if you can't be happy, make sure you keep it your own little secret."

The punch was left untouched while they sat across the table from each other, their eyes locked in silent combat.

"One more thing," Momma said. "In case you may have neglected to buy a wedding present, you still have time to take a horseback ride up to the store. When you've finished with the chairs, I'll pay you for your help. Anything you'd like to say for yourself?"

"Yeah, I have somethin' to say," Norman answered. "Why you still calling her Glinnis Quince, when her name ain't Quince anymore? And you don't need to pay me nothing, not one red cent. Kent and me went in together yesterday and bought 'em a sugar bowl with little pink posies windin' around all over it. We didn't get no wrapping paper though. You got any you could lend us? We'll pay you back when we get into town next Saturday."

His gaze didn't falter, but my mother's did. It shifted to a nebulous spot on the kitchen floor. Then she laughed and went into her bedroom. It was the first time I'd seen her laugh in several weeks. When she came back with a sheet of white tissue paper, she was still laughing. By that time, Norman and I were laughing too.

"It doesn't do me one bit of good to get mad at you, Norman Hibbard!" Momma said. "No matter how hard I try, I can never make it last."

Kent Williamson's real father had floated into my imagination in a number of various forms, all of them unattractive in one way or another. I didn't expect him to look like normal, everyday people. But he did.

"Pleased to meet you," he said shyly, extending his hand to my dad.

"Glad to meet *you*," my father answered. "Follow me, and I'll show you the room you'll be staying in. Right through here."

He led Mr. Williamson into my bedroom. I would be sleeping on the front room couch for the night. Actually, the man didn't look like just anybody else. He looked like a taller Kent Williamson, which, in itself, made it impossible for me to dislike him the way I'd planned to. I looked for some sign of evil, distinguishing features, but there were none. He just appeared to be awfully nervous. He was much younger than I'd imagined, and more robust.

"It's mighty good of you folks to let me stay the night," he said. "I could have spent the night in town in the hotel, I guess, but it sure is nicer being out here where I'll have a chance to visit the boy."

"We're glad to have you," my father said. "No use staying in a hotel room all by yourself. It's not a very friendly place to be."

"It's real obliging of you to invite the boy to supper too. Give us a chance to get acquainted."

It seemed odd to hear Mr. Williamson constantly speak of his own son as "the boy"; the term was so formal-sounding. I wished he'd call him by his given name.

"We'd be glad to have Kent anytime," my father replied, as if in answer to my thought. "He's a fine young man. You can be mighty proud of him, Mr. Williamson."

"Well, I am proud. It done my heart good to see he's turned into such a good-acting fellow," Mr. Williamson said. "By the way, why don't you just call me Nyle?"

"I'd like to; never do feel comfortable 'mistering' around," my father said. He reached down and scooted his chair forward, a sign that he was about to delve into more serious business.

"This must be a real hard thing for you to go through, Nyle," he said. "I imagine it's pretty rough."

"It is," Mr. Williamson said. "But I know it's best for the boy. That isn't what's bothering me the most. The worst part is, I know I haven't done right by him, and there's no way to make up for it."

My father had no answer for this. He fidgeted and fixed his attention on the piping of the chair arm he was rubbing with his thumbs.

"And it's nobody's fault but mine. It's just too late, that's all. I been married again, now, for a lot of years. And sad to say, my wife really don't want anything to do with the boy. We've got three of our own."

"I see," my father said.

I didn't see. I didn't see at all.

"You know, sometimes your life just seems to get out of hand, and you don't know why or what to do about it. Things happen . . . "

Engrossed in their conversation, the two men had not noticed Kent crossing the road that very minute. I didn't want him to hear what his father was saying, so I hurried out to meet him.

Momma and I cleared the pudding bowls off the table and started to finish up the dishes. My father had announced his intention of going out to check on the livestock in order to give Nyle Williamson a chance to talk to his son alone, but surprisingly Kent's father had requested that Dad join them in the living room. We could hear their male voices over the clattering of silverware.

"And I want to be baptized. I'm planning on being baptized right away," Kent said.

"Do you have any problem with that, Nyle?" my father asked.

"No. None at all. I wish I'd been baptized when I was a boy. I never did know anything about religion; wasn't brought up to. But I never heard of a little religion doing anything but good."

Momentarily there was no sound but our clattering of plates. Then Kent said, "I'd like to know one thing, Pa, just one. How you could have gone off and left me when my ma died."

Mr. Williamson coughed. "Well, you had your grandma, and she didn't care too much for me. I talked your mother into getting married too young. Neither one of us was quite sixteen years old. I didn't think we were too young at the time. I thought I knew everything. At that age, I thought I could make anything I wanted happen, just by making up my mind to it."

He sighed deeply and continued: "Oh, my—was I ever young! Your grandma had no use for me whatever, and I can't say as I blame her. She thought it was my fault your ma died. She felt so bad she couldn't think straight. She wouldn't let me have you. The law went along with her."

As I stacked plates in the cupboard and listened, my mind started to change in regard to Nyle Williamson.

"I couldn't fight it. I was too young and inexperienced to even know how to start. So after a few weeks, I just took off—decided I'd go as far away as I could get. It wasn't right. If I had it to do over, I'd have stuck around and waited."

"Well, don't you want me now?"

"Oh, son! Son . . . I do! Believe me, I do. But I've got a whole other life. My new wife—well, she has some serious thinking problems. And I have three other kids."

"What are they?" Kent asked. "Boys or girls? I'd like to know."

"Well, the oldest two are girls. Then I've got one little boy."

"They're my sisters. They're my sisters and my brother. I think I have a right to get to know them, don't you?" Kent said.

"Maybe. Since you put it that way, I guess maybe you do. But you moving in wouldn't work. Believe me. Believe me, boy. I know what I'm talking about."

"Someday, someday soon," Kent said, "I mean to meet my sisters and brother."

I had not the shadow of a doubt in my mind but what he would. I glanced over at Momma. She had got her stationery box out and was folding papers.

"Now, I want you to tell me their names," he went on.

"Joan and Julie and Dennis."

"Joan. Julie. Dennis." Kent formed the words slowly and softly.

"No, boy," Mr. Williamson said, resuming the former conversation, "I have nothing against you gettin' baptized. Or living with those Hibbard folks. They want to adopt you legal, it seems. But I'm hoping one thing. I'm hoping you won't change your name."

"I never thought of it. Getting adopted doesn't mean you have to change your name, does it, Mr. Borden?" Kent asked.

"I wouldn't think so."

"Well, I don't want to. I won't change my name. It's who I am."

"I'm sure there's a way for the Hibbards to get legal custody without you having to change your name, son," my father said. "Otherwise, there'd be no justice."

After Kent had gone back over to the Hibbards', my mother and father stayed up a little longer, talking to Nyle Williamson.

"What is that boy, now? Twelve, thirteen years old? It's a stern age," my father said. "When he's older, he might see your side of it better."

"I hope so. There's just not a thing I can do."

My mother walked over to Mr. Williamson and handed him the folded stationery and some envelopes.

"I've addressed these envelopes ahead of time," she said. "And I've stamped them. All you need to do is sit down and write a few words every week or so. That's something you can do."

Nyle Williamson took the stationery. "I will," he said. "I promise you. I'll keep in touch with the boy."

I remembered my cousin, Audra, saying the very same thing.

Near the end of September, Kent Williamson was baptized in the canal by the meetinghouse bridge. A number of Wind Valley Ward members were there, Lillian Brownstone among them. She had made him a new dark blue suit for his confirmation that was as good as anything done by a tailor in New York City or Paris, France.

126

The essence of summer crystallized. Leaves fell from the cottonwoods, forming rustling tawny heaps under the massive, sturdy trunks. Potato vines flattened into brown, brittle stalks that reached out and met each other between rows. Wheat stubble gleamed golden and mellow under a miraculously blue depth of sky. And the water rippled its imperturbable, endless hymn.

Chapter

11

Every year in October we were dismissed from school for two weeks to help with the potato harvest. We could usually dig all my father's spuds in one week and then hire out to another farmer the second week. These harvest earnings were our main source of spending money for the entire winter.

My mother generally stood on the narrow platform across from me on the combine. But this year my father hired Grace Jacobson to help pull the vines. Norman Hibbard bagged the potatoes as they came over the combine and set the bags out in the field to be bucked onto the truck by Clayton Hibbard—who traded work with my father—and stacked on the truck bed by Kent Williamson. Jack straightened gunny sacks and picked loose spuds off the ground for our winter storage. Momma stayed at home this year with Billy and cooked magnificent midday dinners for all the hands.

Clothes that were piled on first thing in the morning to

brave the frost-covered fields were peeled off, layer by layer, until by noon we were sweating under the strong rays of sun in our shirtsleeves.

My father drove digger, urging the horses on from time to time with a clicking of his tongue and a sharp snap of the reins. Harvest brought a feeling of richness and beauty all its own. It was a season of intensified perception, of absolute attunement. The very earth seemed to breathe through us.

"What say we have a little break?" Dad suggested, reining in the horses. "I'm dry as a bone. Nola, run get that jar of water from under the willow tree over there, will you?"

Everyone started taking off their gloves, pounding the dust out of them as they sought a resting place in the shade. The men pushed back their caps and wiped their foreheads on the sleeves of their shirts.

My father grinned as he unscrewed the lid and passed around the Mason jar. The water had the vague taste of rubber from the lid.

"Well, we ought to finish this field today, folks," he said. "Just one more patch across the canal and we'll be all done, and you can all go out and make your fortunes."

The trucking crew stopped too. Glinnis Hibbard was driving, and she got out of the truck and came over with us, as did Clay and Kent.

"Brought some cookies," she said, passing around a paper bag. "Have some."

I noticed Norman wasn't glaring at her any more. When she got to him she handed him a dark blue bandana. "Here," she said. "You forgot this."

"Thanks," he said, tieing it around his neck so he'd have it when he needed to ward off the dust. He actually came close to smiling at her.

Kent joined Grace and me at our spot under the willow trees.

"Boy, this shade feels good!" he said. "Wish I could sit here all afternoon."

He popped a cookie into his mouth whole, reached into his back pocket, and pulled out a well-worn envelope. From that he extracted a piece of folded paper and began to read.

"Who's the letter from?" I asked.

"Oh, just somebody," he answered, frowning. He folded the paper, replaced it in the envelope, and put it back into his pocket, but not before I got a really good look at it. It was one of my mother's Irish-linen ones, the kind she had given to Nyle Williamson.

An immense moon hung in the sky the night of our bonfire. From the field near the house we'd raked spud vines into a huge pile for burning and the accompanying ritual of the potato roast. This was the official end of the harvest as far as we were concerned. Each year we dug a pit lined with rocks and filled with spuds over which we built a roaring fire which would eventually cook them, at least half-way.

This year, because prices were good and no potatoes had been frozen in the ground, my father had given us the bonus of the makings of hot dogs and marshmallows to roast over the fire on whittled sticks. I removed the black remnants of a marshmallow that had caught on fire.

"Is your real father still writing to you?" I asked Kent Williamson, as I licked my fingers.

"Who told you he was sending me letters?"

"Oh, nobody. I just know."

"Well, yes. I've got three of them, so far."

"Do you always answer?"

"Sure," he said, after he'd swallowed his mouthful of hot dog. "I send one off the next day."

I knew Kent was a private person, but I couldn't quell my curiosity any longer.

"What kind of things does he write about?"

"Oh, for one thing, he says that after the way everybody treated him so good here, he went out and bought a Bible and started reading it."

"What else does he say?" I asked.

Kent didn't answer, so I asked again.

"He says that girls ought to mind their own business and not keep sticking their noses into other people's."

I was mentally preparing an indignant rebuttal to this insult when I saw the face of my father, illuminated by firelight. He walked over and stood behind me, his hands on his hips. After he'd looked into the flames for a minute, he said quietly, so that only I could hear, "Well, guess we're gonna have to let the fire die down now. Looks like it's time to take your mother to the hospital."

Of all the astonishing aspects of this small and beautiful creature, there was one I really couldn't stop marveling at—those amazing fingernails. To think there would be little creases in the knuckles, too. And a little bud of a mouth that already knew how to suckle.

I could have held her in my arms all day long, and did a great deal of the time, because of Billy. I couldn't imagine how Billy could keep from adoring her as much as the rest of us, but he was downright hateful, and Momma had to spend a lot of time holding him on her lap. That suited me fine.

My fondest dream had come true. After all those boys I'd had to contend with through the years, I finally had a girl all my own. Well, in a way all my own. When I wasn't holding her, I spent my spare time sewing pink ribbons on the nightgowns I'd helped Momma make for her. We'd waited to see whether we got a boy or a girl before finishing them.

She had such a sweet smell, too. A kind of special baby

perfume. And when you held out a finger, she took hold of it.

"Land, you're going to have that baby so spoiled that when you're in school your mother won't be able to get a thing done," my grandmother said.

"No, I won't," I said. "Patricia never cries; only when she's hungry." The baby had been named after my grandfather, at least as nearly as possible.

"Well, if she isn't spoiled, it won't be because you didn't try."

I knew this was just talk. Grandma spoiled her as much as I did.

"Well, Ma," my mother said, "I wish you'd stay on with us—for good. You're going to get awfully lonesome this winter all by yourself."

"Maybe someday you'll have to have me," Grandma answered, "but let's not rush things. I'll be all right. Rob and Kate come by every few days, and your Uncle John and Aunt Iris look in on me for a few minutes nearly every evening."

"Still," Momma said, "I worry."

"Well, stop worrying. Besides, I'm sort of selfish, I guess; I like to live in my own place. I've got my church work and I'm on the school board and the Democrats are after me constantly to do work for them. I don't have time to get too lonely. Besides, if I lived with you, where would you go when Saturday afternoon rolled around?"

Momma sighed. "I guess I'm selfish, too. I like you here," she said.

Grandma patted her hand. "You'll be all right. Being apart is what makes us so glad to see each other. I've always felt lucky to be welcomed here. I honestly have the feeling Frank likes me. Not every mother-in-law can say that. I want to keep it that way."

Patricia was asleep. As carefully as anything, I got up and put her in her basket.

133

"Besides, you've got plenty of good help right there," Grandma said, nodding in my direction.

We packed her things out to Uncle Rob's car and, after visiting with Uncle Rob and Aunt Kate for a few minutes, told them all good-bye. After they had driven slowly down the lane and around the corner, we lingered momentarily, savoring the out-of-doors.

Even with the sun out in the middle of the afternoon it was chilly now. The days were shortening. But thousands of miles away, across the Pacific Ocean, the same sunlight fell balmy and serene on Pearl Harbor. Here and there it glinted briefly on the *Oklahoma* and the *Nevada*.

Thanksgiving dinner was over. We'd eaten roast duck and dressing and potatoes and gravy and Lillian Brownstone's canned beans smothered in bacon bits till food was coming out of our ears.

"Who wants squash pie? There's fruitcake, too," my mother announced.

My father, in his unvarying post-holiday-dinner speech, replied, "Afraid I'll have to let the rest of my grub settle a couple of hours before I can take on my dessert. No space left, not one square inch," he added, patting his stomach. "You're just too good a cook, Louise, that's all there is to it."

I missed Grandpa. Everybody did, I knew. But in the place where he usually sat beside my grandmother, Momma had put the baby's basket on a chair. Of course, Patricia hadn't taken Grandpa's place; nobody could. But still, the spot was filled and didn't leave a sad, empty space.

"Anybody else?" Momma asked. "Anybody else want dessert?"

"I hate to be the only one," Grandma answered, "but maybe I will have just a sliver of pie. I like to end a meal with a taste of sweet."

"I'll have a sliver too," I said.

My father leaned back in his chair, chewing on a tooth-pick. "We've had quite a summer," he said.

"We sure have," Momma replied, setting the plates of pie down in front of Grandma and me. "Almost enough summer to last a lifetime."

"Well, at least things turned out just fine for the Williamson boy—he's fitting in over there like a regular trooper; you'd think he'd been around forever."

It seemed natural, now, for Kent to be living with the Hibbards. I was even getting used to Glinnis Quince being a part of the household across the road.

"Speaking of the Hibbards," Momma said, "I've invited them over to visit and play games. Lillian Brownstone, too. She's taken over as Kent Williamson's grandmother—has even got him to call her 'Granny,' I hear. They'll be coming over around five-thirty or six. I guess we'd better get these dishes done so we'll be ready to set the games up."

When we'd finished putting the house back in order, the Hibbard family still had not arrived.

"I think I'll go out for a walk," I told Momma. "I'll keep an eye on the Hibbards' place, and come back in by the time they're ready."

Whenever I'd been cooped up with a crowd for very long, I liked to do that—get out in the fresh air and wander and think about things. I liked to be out close to the fields and talk to my own mind.

I walked down the familiar road, now rutted and hard with frost. I looked up into the trees that lined the lane. Every leaf was gone from the cottonwoods. Their branches were stripped and stark against the sky. Wild geese formed a precise V-shaped soaring image overhead, flying toward the hills to the south. Above them, austere, bleached clouds hinted of snow. I could feel winter hunkering down.

I walked until the sky began to darken, consciously trying to store the summer, this moment, in my memory, trying to keep the look of the fallow fields, the huddling cattle, the smoke curling in wisps from the chimneys. Then the wind came up, and I turned around and headed back toward the beckoning lights of home.

The Hibbards were already there, laughing and talking in the front room. I hung my coat in its place on a hook by the door. On the kitchen table by a smear of whipped cream one lone plate sat, empty of pie. I moved it and wiped the oilcloth clean. When it had dried, I unfolded the checker board and laid it down, making sure it was squared off exactly to the table edge, straight as a string, the way my grandfather would have done.